THE ROGUE AND THE JEWEL

A Regency Historical Romance

ROGUES OF THE ROAD

SASHA COTTMAN

Copyright © 2021 by Sasha Cottman

All rights reserved.

No part of this book may be reproduced in any form or by any electronic or mechanical means, including information storage and retrieval systems, without written permission from the author, except for the use of brief quotations in a book review.

To Sharon, The Book Queen

Chapter One

❦

"Where is my pistol? I had it just a minute ago."

It couldn't have disappeared. Gus Jones frantically stuffed his hand into the pocket of his jacket, searching for the weapon, sighing with relief when his fingers touched cool metal. The gun was right where he had left it.

You dolt. How many times a day do you have to check for it?

Another anxious moment which had set his heart racing. The need to constantly have a loaded pistol close at hand was an odd response for someone who had so recently been shot.

There couldn't be many safer places than his family's home in London. In addition to that was the fact that the man who had tried to kill him was over two hundred miles away in France. But even the deep blue waters of the English Channel couldn't separate Gus from the painful memories of that day at Château-de-La-Roche, when a bullet had very nearly ended his life.

I am home, and I am safe.

These panic attacks made no sense; then again, they never had. The mind was a strange beast. You could tell yourself all the sensible things in the world but fear always lurked in dark recesses.

"You must focus on the task at hand," he chided himself.

Seated on the dusty floor of the cramped attic, he was taking an inventory of his weapons cache. Over the years, it had built to quite an impressive collection: pistols, rifles, and a compelling set of death-wielding knives.

There was also enough gunpowder to give his mother nightmares if she ever discovered what her third-eldest son had hidden in the space above her sitting room.

He really ought to have stored all of it at the RR Coaching Company offices in Gracechurch Street rather than here. If the explosives did go up, the family home would be reduced to rubble.

But despite his better judgement, Gus had continued to bring his ill-gotten arsenal home with him.

Home.

What were the chances he would ever see this place again?

The eve of battle always gave a man reason to consider his life choices. To question exactly the point where he had gone wrong. Only a fool willingly took up arms and went to start a war.

Augustus Trajan Jones had arrived at so many of these crossroads in his nine and twenty years that it was nigh on impossible for him to decipher which of the paths taken had led him to where he now stood.

What was clear, however, was his duty to help Armand and Evangeline La Roche. To do all he could to save them both from a senseless death.

As he leaned over and picked up a single-barreled H.W. Mortimer shotgun from the floor, Evangeline's letter crinkled in his jacket pocket. It was a letter he had read many times.

Dear Augustus,
If you are reading this letter, then you are not dead.
Things have gone from bad to worse since you left.

My uncle has gathered a large store of weapons at the château.
He means to go to war with the Lamballe gang and will not listen to me.
Please do not return to Saint-Brieuc—it is no longer safe.
Evangeline

He knew exactly why he was still carrying it weeks after it had arrived, long after he had memorized its contents. The missive had come from her.

The relationship between him and Evangeline was complicated. It always had been. But a near-death experience could give a man reason to reassess his priorities.

If Armand La Roche was determined to go to war against a rival smuggling gang in France, then Gus most certainly would be standing alongside him when the first volley was fired. He wasn't deterred by Evangeline's express command that he shouldn't come.

If she hadn't wanted me to travel to Saint-Brieuc, she wouldn't have written.

He tested the gun sights then set the rifle aside. Every piece of weaponry laid out before him had been oiled, polished, and checked.

It took some effort, but he struggled to his feet, wincing as his slowly healing chest wound protested.

Will this thing ever fully heal?

It had been six pain-filled weeks since his fellow rogue of the road, Sir Stephen Moore, had carried the badly injured Gus on board the *Night Wind*.

There were times he woke in the dark soaked in nightmare-induced sweat. He could only pray that eventually the memory of being held down while Captain Grey dug into his flesh with a heated blade would fade. They had saved his life, but the sound of his own screams still echoed in his head.

He rubbed at the wound. A dose of laudanum would be

most welcome, but Gus didn't like the way the drug addled his brain. Pain kept a man's mind sharp. It reminded him of the cost of poor decisions.

Lifting his left arm, he raised it as high as the injury would allow. The bullet fired by one of the members of Vincent Marec's gang had gone deep into the upper section of his chest, chipping off a piece of his clavicle.

There was every chance he would never again have the full use of his arm.

If I survive this next trip, I am likely going to have to retire the boat—find another way to make a living.

Over the past year or so, other members of the rogues of the road—Harry, George, and more recently, Stephen—had made the monumental decision to step away from a life of illicit dealings. All three of them were working at honest careers and had taken on wives. Only Gus and Monsale now remained embedded in their criminal endeavors, both still bachelors.

Monsale wouldn't ever change his life for a woman.

But could I?

He wasn't as set against marriage as his friend Stephen had once been, but it would take a rare lady to consider throwing her lot in with a smuggler. To know that every time her husband sailed from Portsmouth, he may not return. Finding a wife like that was proving to be a tall ask.

Gus was still staring at the weapons cache, unsure as to how much of the gunpowder he should take, when the partly ajar door swung fully open.

His father retired naval captain, William Jones, stepped into the room. He huffed and quickly closed the door behind him. Captain Jones pointed at the key in the lock. "You really should keep that turned. If any of the household servants stumble across this lot, they will surely run and tell your mother. And then there will be no living with her."

Gus scowled. He couldn't ever have the door closed, let

alone locked. The attic was small; and he didn't have a good relationship with enclosed spaces.

"You know I can't do that, sir," he replied.

His father hummed his obvious disapproval. "Augustus, you are a grown man. Only children are frightened of such things."

Gus did his best to ignore the comment, having lost count of the number of times he and his father had argued over his irrational fear. It had been his main reason for not following his father into the navy. The idea of being stuck below deck with a hundred other bodies filled him with dread.

"Have you come to see me with a purpose in mind?".

His father's gaze roamed over the various weapons and crates of ammunition. "So, you are still determined to go to France? Damn. I was hoping you might change your mind."

Gus could well understand his sire's predicament. If he didn't make it back to England alive, Captain Jones was going to be left with a lot of explaining to do.

Father and son had a private understanding of what Gus had been up to both during the war and subsequent years. And while the captain had made his thoughts on the topic of smuggling quite clear, he was not about to turn his son over to the authorities.

"I have to go. They need me. The Lamballe gang are not just some local fisherman's collective who have decided they want a cut of the smuggling trade. From what Armand and Evangeline have told me, Marec is a skilled former French army officer. He knows how to lead."

His father glanced at Gus's damaged shoulder. "And his men are crack shots with a rifle."

Gus's hopes for hiding at the Duke of Monsale's residence and keeping his injury secret from his family had not lasted long. Captain Jones had been on the doorstep of Monsale House within a day of the badly wounded Gus returning to London. News of his arrival into Portsmouth Harbor had passed quickly through the network of retired naval officers and all the way to his sire.

His father laid a hand on his good shoulder. "Who else is going with you?"

Blast. I was hoping to avoid that question.

He steeled himself. "No one. Just the crew. Harry's wife is due to give birth any day. Stephen's blushing bride gave up her wedding night when he came with me last time, so I would not dare ask him again. And George swore a vow to Jane that his days of dirty deeds were behind him. They have all officially retired from the business of being rogues."

"And Monsale?"

Gus reluctantly met his father's gaze.

"You know full well he will not dare set foot in France. And I wouldn't ever ask it of him. This is my quest; and I shall not have the arrest and execution of a friend on my conscience," replied Gus.

Captain Jones pulled his son into his embrace. "And I don't suppose threatening to tell your mother the truth of the things you have been up to all these years would do me any good either?"

Gus closed his eyes and let his father's words wash over him. Lying to his mother had never sat well with him but having her know the truth would be far worse. He would much prefer that she continued to think him an honest sailor.

"No, it wouldn't." He accepted a second hug then drew back. "I had better finish up here and then go make arrangements to have the weapons I am taking to France collected. The rest of the RR Coaching Company want to have a directors' meeting early tomorrow before I leave, so I won't have time in the morning."

"Alright, but could you at least promise me one thing?"

He forced himself to meet his father's eyes. "Name it."

"If there comes a point where you have the choice between being a bloody hero or setting aside your pride and living another day, please think of your mother. She doesn't deserve to spend the rest of her days grieving over you. And neither do I, for that matter."

Gus swallowed the lump in his throat. He couldn't blame his father for using guilt to try to make him stay. He would have done exactly the same. "You drive a hard bargain, sir, but yes. I promise not to throw my life away too cheaply. I shall keep myself constrained when it comes to heroics."

He had no intention of ever letting Vincent Marec and his men win. As far as he was concerned, the Lamballe gang would still be counting the cost of having attacked both the château and his crew long after he had finished with them. Revenge was going to be swift and complete.

His mission to France was twofold: save Evangeline and Armand, while settling a deadly score.

Chapter Two

※

Château-de-La-Roche
Saint-Brieuc, France

The cool breeze from the Gouët river ruffled Evangeline's long, brown locks. In what her late mother would have considered an act of impetuous rebellion, she had untied the ribbon her maid had carefully threaded through her hair and let the wind have its way.

While the knotted plaits had come free with ease, she couldn't say the same for the tight fists of worry which sat heavily in her stomach.

What am I to do?

She glanced back in the direction of the château. The spire of the central turret peeked out over the top of the pine trees. This place had been her home, her sanctuary for many years, yet today it felt anything but safe.

Strangers were moving about the yard, carrying boxes and cases of heavens knew what into the west wing. Armand wouldn't tell her anything. He had even locked her out of several parts of the house, including the formal dining room.

When she spied the fifth cart rolling up the road, Evangeline had given up watching and come down to the water's edge, seeking solace. But even her favorite place couldn't calm the torment in her mind.

Armand was making ready to go to war against Vincent Marec.

"He knows nothing about fighting, whereas Vincent is a battle-hardened warrior," she muttered.

If she didn't do something to stop her uncle, they were all going to end up dead.

She turned and fixed her gaze on the dark turquoise waters of the English Channel, scanning the horizon for any sign of a ship.

Not just any ship.

From the first morning after she had sent the letter to Gus Jones, Evangeline had looked out to sea, hoping to see the *Night Wind* sail into view.

But nothing. Hope was fading.

Did it even reach him?

Her last sight of Gus had been as Sir Stephen Moore helped carry him on board the yacht. He had been seriously injured—shot by one of Vincent's men.

She winced at the memory of Gus falling in a crumpled heap to the ground, her own cries echoing among the trees as he collapsed. And then the blood. As the front of his linen shirt ran crimson with his life force, Evangeline's worry had turned to dread.

How they had managed to get him on the back of her horse, she couldn't recall. Her mind had been stripped of everything but pure fear. Even now, she couldn't be certain that Gus was still alive.

I wish someone would send word. I hate this not knowing.

Seeing the English smuggler so badly hurt had finally crystallized her feelings for him. For a long while now, every time his yacht docked at the small jetty at the bottom of the hill, she had waited impatiently for him to make his way up to the château. Had even felt a sense of jealousy over her uncle ushering Gus down to the cellars to show him the latest shipment of brandy which he was to take back to Portsmouth.

And as much as she had tried to deny it, the curious sensations all had one root cause. The rugged rogue had stolen her heart.

"What am I going to do?" she muttered.

Romantic notions of Gus Jones were not, however, one of her current priorities. Staying alive and keeping their home was paramount.

All attempted negotiations with the Lamballe gang had ceased months ago. Hostilities between them had increased to such a state that she was now firmly convinced that only a bloody battle would finally see one of them emerge the victor.

Closing her eyes, she sent a silent prayer to her dead parents. "Please let help arrive."

When she looked again, the sea and the horizon beyond was still empty of ships. Disappointed, she turned and headed back to the château. Hoping and praying wasn't working.

As Evangeline reached the top of the rise and stepped onto the gravel of the main courtyard, she immediately wished she had stayed at the beach.

A large black stallion stood next to the entrance to the stables. It was a beast of a horse, at least seventeen hands. Only one man in the local area owned such a mount. Vincent Marec.

"*Merde*," she whispered.

Any plans she might have had to backtrack and not be seen quickly evaporated.

"There you are! Armand's *économe*. I was wondering where you were hiding."

Rude as always. There was not the slightest chance that Vincent might consider addressing her as Mademoiselle La

Roche. No. As far as he was concerned, she was her uncle's housekeeper, nothing more.

The thought of what else Marec had made plain he wished Evangeline to be sent a shiver down her spine.

Never. I would rather die.

"What do you want, Vincent?" she snapped. Bravado was one of the few weapons she had at her disposal.

The tall, heavily built Vincent approached her, arms held out wide. The smile on his face did little to hide the obvious price his body was paying for a life of heavy drinking and lechery. "Come now. Is that any way to greet a friend? Or an old lover?"

Evangeline gritted her teeth. She had made a mistake long ago, and Vincent was determined to remind her of it every time they met.

"Perhaps I should wave a gun in your face. That seems to be the only sort of reception that you understand," she replied.

Vincent tutted. "Like how you shot at Claude? He is not a happy man. You put a hole in his best hat."

She was sorely tempted to make mention of the fact that Claude had been the one who shot Gus but thought the better of it. Starting an argument would not see Vincent leave any time soon, and she needed him gone. The longer he remained, the less safe she felt.

"Where is Armand?" he demanded.

Evangeline shook her head. Vincent wasn't one for wasting time with people who didn't serve a purpose. And when it came to women, he only wanted them for one thing.

"I don't know. I have been down at the cove," she replied.

Vincent gave a huff of annoyance. "Well, you tell him that I called in on my way to town. And that I expect an answer within the next few days." He nodded in the direction of a nearby wagon. "You should be able to fit your belongings in that cart, so he has no excuse. Feel free to leave the furniture."

If the volume of weapons and ammunition Armand had been gathering and storing in the cellars below the stables was any indication, Evangeline was certain that her uncle's answer was still a firm no. He was not going to let the Lamballe gang have free rein over the smuggling trade in this part of Brittany. Nor was he going to quietly give up the château.

She followed Vincent as he leisurely strolled over to the cart.

"I shall tell Armand you were here, now will you please leave?"

He stood for a moment at the open end of the wagon, then bent and ran his hand across the wooden bed. He sniffed at the black powder on his fingertips. "Gunpowder? Now what use would your uncle have for such a thing?"

This could be trouble.

"Wild boar. They have been digging up some of the household crops. Armand plans to shoot them and then hang their carcasses up to warn off any others that might stray into the grounds," she replied.

It wasn't a complete fabrication. Wild boars had been at the kitchen garden. She had even managed to shoot one herself.

He shrugged his shoulders. "Just make sure you kill them all before my men and I return. We will need the garden. I like a few herbs in my soup."

She turned to walk away, but Vincent roughly seized her by the arm and pulled her to him. "Tell Armand he shouldn't be so careless with his powder. In the army, I would have had a man under my command beaten for such waste."

He put his finger under her chin and lifted. When Evangeline tried to turn her head away, he gripped her face firmly with his hand. She stared into his cold, gray eyes as he wiped his thumb over her lips, smearing gunpowder all over them.

"You made a mistake in refusing me a second time. But I

am a patient man; and when you and Armand are homeless, you might rethink your position. Women who are foolish enough to say no to me, always come to regret their decision. Evangeline, your future is by my side, quiet and obedient."

She pulled away the instant he released his hold.

"I will never yield to a man like you, Vincent Marec."

❧

Evangeline waited until Vincent and his horse had disappeared from sight before going in search of Armand. She found him and two of the estate workers in the cellar at the back of the stables. They were busy throwing straw over cases of gunpowder, and that had her worried.

This place rivals the Bastille for ammunition.

She could only pray that her home didn't suffer the same fate of being stormed and seized by an angry mob.

Armand raised his head as Evangeline approached. "Has he gone?"

"You knew Vincent was here? You should have come out and confronted him, rather than leaving it up to me," she huffed.

"As I recall, you are the one who has spent the best part of the last few months telling me that you are more than capable of dealing with the Lamballe gang."

He motioned toward the door and the estate laborers quickly left. The château servants and staff had of late become well acquainted with the need to make themselves scarce whenever instructed. There were not many smiling faces to be seen about the château.

Her uncle was, of course, right. She had made it clear that she wasn't afraid of Vincent. But the fact that Armand had chosen not to face the gang boss gave her cause for concern.

What are you hiding, Uncle?

With still no word from England, she couldn't wait any

longer for help to arrive. It was time to confront Armand. "Uncle, I am worried. Please tell me what you have planned. I am not a fool. I know you intend to refuse Vincent's demands, but you still haven't told me what all this weaponry and ammunition is for."

"And I don't intend to tell you. Please understand, Evangeline, it is the only way I can keep you safe. That is what matters."

Evangeline threw up her hands. "What about you? Have you even considered the possibility that Vincent might be prepared to kill in order to get what he wants?"

She could have cheerfully slapped Armand when he gifted her with one of his patronizing, *I am your uncle* looks. "Don't worry. I have plans well in place. The only thing Marec will be getting out of this argument is a burial plot in Saint-Michel cemetery."

He pointed to the black marks on her face. "You should go fix your face and hair then check to see what is for supper. That is the kind of life for a woman like you, Evangeline. Not getting involved in arguments with men like Marec. I promise, the next time he comes here, I shall deal with him."

And that's the problem. You don't have the faintest idea how to handle a man like Vincent. You can't even manage simple negotiations over the price of brandy without me telling you exactly what to do.

Her uncle was out of his depth and headed into peril. And there was nothing she could do to stop the tragedy which was surely coming.

Chapter Three

The journey from London to Portsmouth would take the best part of two days. In the early stages of the smuggling operation, Gus had made the strategic decision to moor the *Night Wind* away from the capital. He had sound reasons.

The first being, it enabled the quick offloading of most of the contraband. A secret warehouse in Portsmouth town registered under a false name had served the RR Coaching Company well. The other option of simply bringing cargo up the River Thames into the London docks was slow-going and also carried with it great risk. Customs authorities noted every arrival and regularly checked ship manifests.

The second and probably most important reason was that the British navy was based out of Portsmouth. A group of hand-picked local scouts was able to keep Gus well-informed as to the movements of naval vessels in and out of port. One didn't ever wish to encounter one of His Majesty's ships at sea, especially not while endeavoring to smuggle a shipment of illicit goods across the English Channel.

The *Night Wind* itself was registered through a complex web of various companies, across four different countries. If anyone decided to go to the effort of tracing its true ownership, they would be surprised to discover that it was, in fact, the property of the French Navy.

Monsale had thought up that little gem.

After bidding a fond farewell to his parents, Gus took the heavily laden travel coach over to the offices of the RR Coaching Company in Gracechurch Street. A few small tasks and he would be on his way.

The sight of four horses tethered outside the stables in the rear yard had him uttering foul words. He had been hoping Monsale wasn't serious about the five of them conducting a company directors' meeting this morning. The leader of the rogues of the road wasn't normally one for rising at such an early hour. All the signs pointed to a difficult encounter.

"Well, best to get this over and done with," he muttered.

Upstairs inside the company offices, he found the rest of the rogues of the road waiting. A sense of dread quickly descended. Instead of occupying their usual seats, lounging around the big central table, they were all standing shoulder to shoulder in front of the fire.

Grim smiles were set hard on each man's face.

"Who died?" asked Gus, aiming for levity.

Harry and George exchanged side glances. Then Harry stepped forward. "No one, and we would like to keep it that way."

I should have known this was coming.

Gus pulled out a chair and dropped into it. If he was going to be on the end of another lecture about not getting himself killed, he may as well be comfortable.

The Duke of Monsale cleared his throat. "We are not here to try to talk you out of travelling to France."

Harry thrust his hand up in the air. "That's not true. I would dearly love to stop you going, so would Alice. She made me promise to beg you not to leave for France. And in her heavily pregnant state I am loath to say no to anything she asks."

Lady Alice Steele was due to give birth any day now. If the state of Lord Harry's fingernails was any indication, he was more than a little nervous at the prospect of becoming a father.

Monsale glared at him, and Harry let his arm drop. "Yes, well, just wait until you are dealing with an expectant wife, then you will understand."

"As I was saying, we know you feel compelled to go. And we understand your reasons. What we want to discuss is what happens if you don't make it back," said Monsale. He was never a man to mince his words.

They had all been involved in various risky and outright dangerous jobs over the past couple of years, but this was the first time one of them was going into a situation where the chances of them not coming home were high. Gus had hoped to avoid this challenging conversation. But he had come prepared.

He reached into the pocket of his greatcoat and withdrew four letters, placing them side by side on the table. Each of the other members of the rogues of the road had one addressed to them.

Stephen sighed. "Bloody hell. Do you really have to go? Can't we pay some mercenaries to deal with this problem, rather than send you?"

Gus shook his head. Sir Stephen had been with him that day at the château. If anyone should be able to understand Gus's need to go back and face the Lamballe gang, it was him. But it wasn't just about settling a score. Evangeline's letter had him genuinely concerned for both her and Armand's safety.

If anything happens to them — to her — I won't be able to live with myself.

He pointed at the letters. "In them you will find a personal message for each one of you. There are also instructions as to what is to happen to the valuables in my flee box," he said.

Under the RR Coaching Company stables was a strong room containing a safe. At one time each member of the company had stored enough money and treasures in their individual flee boxes to be able to fund an escape from England. Monsale had insisted on them setting up this form of personal insurance.

As various members of the group had subsequently married and given up their criminal careers, the boxes had been retired. Now only Monsale and Gus still maintained them.

He had spent many hours poring over the letters, writing, and then changing them. How did you pen a note to someone who would only ever read it if you were dead?

In the end, Gus had taken out much of the sentimental passages and simply asked that his friends get violently drunk once a year on the anniversary of his demise. To his way of thinking, the dead didn't have the right to dictate how others should grieve for them.

He got to his feet. "Gentlemen, I think that is all that needs to be said."

The long journey to the coast was going to be tough enough without brooding over emotional goodbyes.

George shook his head. "Well, if there is to be no speeches, then at least a drink between friends to wish you good luck is in order."

Monsale grabbed a bottle of rum from the sideboard and poured them all a generous glass. He handed one to Gus. "I stole this from a private party at Admiralty House last summer. I thought it appropriate that we all share it now."

Gus laughed. Only one of the wealthiest men in all of Britain would think it a lark to pilfer rum from the navy.

Heaven help you if they ever discover what else you have stolen from them.

At least Monsale would be spared the ignominy of facing

an ordinary criminal court. Dukes had the long-standing privilege of a trial before their peers in the House of Lords.

The five of them gathered round and raised their glasses. All eyes fell on Gus.

"A toast to the worst group of rogues I have ever had the displeasure to work with. Gentlemen, it has been both an honor and an utter disgrace to know you all."

The lump of emotion in his throat went down with the rum. He set the glass onto the table then, without risking a glance back at his friends, Gus headed for the door.

France and his fate awaited him.

Chapter Four

In the end, Gus packed as many of the guns and powder he thought could be safely stowed on board the *Night Wind*. Gunpowder wasn't something he was keen to carry in large amounts, as ships had a nasty habit of burning to the waterline whenever ammunition caught fire. But if they were going to sail into trouble, he wanted the crew to at least have a chance of being able to make an escape.

The weapons were stored beneath a false floor inside the travel coach. The gunpowder was in small crates under the benches.

If any of the local militia patrolling the London to Portsmouth road were to stop and inquire as to the destination of the carriage, they would simply find a gentleman en route to his friend's house in the country to study the birdlife. Gus had even packed a book on ornithology to complete the look.

He spent the night at Moore Manor, Stephen's estate in Surrey, polishing off an orphaned bottle of whisky he happened to liberate from a locked cupboard, then continued on to Portsmouth the following day.

As the coach reached the top of the rise before beginning

the long descent to the harbor, he dropped open the glass on the door and let the sea breeze in.

A smile sat on his lips. There was nothing better than the salty tang of the ocean; it filled his lungs and cheered his soul.

Dark times may lay ahead, but for now, he was content to enjoy the promise of setting sail with the evening tide. A man was only truly free when it was just himself and the wide blue sea.

His good humor lasted all the way to the dockside—though not as far as his boat.

A stony-faced Captain Grey was waiting for him at the entrance to the jetty. "Thank god you have finally arrived."

Gus frowned. "And a good evening to you too. I am well recovered, thank you for asking."

Captain Grey nodded in the direction of several of the *Night Wind's* usual crew. From the crossed arms and defiant-looking stances, they were clearly not happy.

"What's wrong?" asked Gus.

"They want more money and a guarantee of not getting killed. After the unpleasantness of our last trip to France, they are not eager to go again."

This was an unwelcome, though not surprising, development. Seeing the owner of your vessel being carried on board with a gunshot wound to his chest did tend to make a man take note. Only a fool wouldn't be having second thoughts.

"Alright, I will talk to them. In fact, I want to speak to all the crew before we sail. No man should be leaving port without understanding that we are headed into serious danger." He headed up the gangplank and signaled for everyone to follow him below deck.

Once the fourteen members of the crew and the ship's captain were assembled, Gus addressed them. "You all know how things went last time. We walked into a trap. I barely escaped with my life. This trip, however, we are taking plenty of weapons and ammunition with us. That being said, I don't expect any of you to follow me into battle. Your job is to protect the boat. If there is any sign of trouble, Captain Grey has my express command to sail away from Château-de-La-Roche."

A loud hubbub of protests and outrage immediately sprang up from the crew. Even the captain rounded on him.

With his tightly fisted hands stuffed in his pockets, Gus waited as patiently as his dislike of cramped, crowded spaces would allow.

When the cries and swearing had simmered down, he spoke again. "If any man does not feel safe in setting sail tonight, then he has my blessing to leave right now. I am willingly going to the aid of Armand and Evangeline La Roche. I may never return to England, and that is my choice. You are all free to make your own."

Captain Grey growled in the direction of two of the crew as they quickly made their way toward the ladder and climbed to the weather deck. "Cowards, you won't ever sail with me again!" he bellowed.

The rest of the gathering mumbled and talked amongst themselves but stayed put.

Gus gritted his teeth. They could safely sail with this number of men, but if anyone else made the decision to depart, things might become difficult. As it was, he would have to help with the sails and navigation, especially as they neared the French coast.

He cleared his throat. "Any man who makes the crossing will receive double the normal payment. If things do go wrong, your family will receive a lump sum settlement from the Duke of Monsale. The articles of Bartholomew Roberts will apply."

While Gus hadn't wanted to accept the offer from his friend, Monsale had insisted. He hadn't ever imagined quoting the rules of death benefit payments drawn up by the pirate Black Bart, but if it gained him a crew, then he was prepared to do it.

Forgive me, father. I know there is nothing honorable in being a pirate, but I must get to France.

The promise of compensation seemed to do the trick. No one else left.

He nodded to Captain Grey. "The ship is under the captain's command as of this minute. I will work alongside the rest of you as a member of the crew until we reach Saint-Brieuc. Take the time now to avail yourself of a gun and shot and store them in a dry and secure place."

Gus headed to the ladder. Captain Grey could deal with any last-minute questions or men who were still in two minds. He needed time alone to gather his thoughts.

And fresh air.

After stepping out onto the deck, Gus made for the bow of the yacht. It faced onto the harbor, affording him his favorite view of blue water. For a moment, he stood staring at one of the nearby ships as its sails billowed in the breeze.

Am I doing the right thing in putting these men's lives in danger just to help my friends? And what if we arrive in France and things are worse than Evangeline said they were—what will I do?

The need to get to Evangeline, to confirm that she was safe, occupied his mind almost constantly. Evangeline La Roche was a strong young woman; she wouldn't have gone to all the trouble of sending a letter to England if she hadn't genuinely feared for her and Armand's well-being.

"If I have to row the whole bloody way myself, I will," he muttered.

Footsteps on the deck had him stirring from his private musings. He glanced back over his shoulder.

Captain Grey stood a few feet away. "Mister Jones, the men are ready to sail to France." He pointed at Gus's left arm. "I don't expect you will be strong enough to help with the sails, but if you could work the ropes, we should be able to leave port without too much difficulty."

Their gazes met. Silence followed. Neither had to give voice to their concerns about the expedition. They were likely sailing into a bloody battle, from which some of them may not return.

"I meant it when I said that you are to leave Saint-Brieuc at the first sign of strife. The Lamballe gang are former soldiers, hardened by war. They have much to gain by taking over the smuggling operations."

Captain Grey scowled, clearly unhappy with Gus's order. "How about we make a pact? If you run into trouble, I shall take the *Night Wind* farther up the French coast to Binic. It's close enough to Saint-Brieuc, and we know people there. I can keep the boat in port for a time. If you don't make it to Binic and signal me there within a week, then I shall sail for England. That is my final offer—take it or leave it."

The idea of being stranded in France with a band of cutthroats on the hunt to kill him held little appeal. If things did go awry, having a way to escape could well mean the difference between life and death.

Gus held out his hand. "You drive a hard bargain, but yes, we are in accord. Now be a good chap and show me which ropes you want hauling; I want us to sail the minute the tide turns."

Chapter Five

✦

Silence was the order as the *Night Wind* drew up alongside the small, private dock below Château-de-La-Roche. The château itself sat at the top of the hill, hidden from view by a cluster of tall pine trees. Only the topmost part of its spire could be seen as they'd sailed up the Gouët river.

It was mid-morning, and the night crossing of the English Channel had gone without incident. Gus was praying that their luck would hold.

While three members of the crew held guns trained on the track leading up to the main house, Gus made ready. He dropped over the side of the yacht and landed on the wooden jetty with a thud.

Loaded pistol in hand, he made for the cover of a nearby cluster of boulders, staying low as he ran. With his back pressed against the rocks, he watched as the crew and captain scanned the surrounding area. When Captain Grey pointed to the path and nodded, Gus crept out from his hiding place and headed up the hill.

He didn't need to look behind him to know that the *Night Wind* was drawing away from the jetty and turning about. If they had to make a hasty exit, they couldn't afford to waste valuable time in getting the boat ready to sail.

His heart was thumping hard in his chest. The last time he stood on the side of this rise, he had been close to death. It took a great deal of effort to push those memories away, to fight the rising panic.

Move. Find Evangeline and Armand.

At the edge of the courtyard leading to the château, he stopped and hid behind a tree. There was little activity about the grounds. A stray chicken wandered out from the kitchen garden, followed by one of the château's housemaids.

Nothing seemed out of place.

The stone walls of the château looked the same as they had always done. As he took in the welcome sight of the round central turret, with its gray slate tiled roof and griffin-topped spire, a grin came to his lips.

It's good to be here again.

He sighed with bone-deep relief as a familiar figure appeared at the main doorway in the center of the château's eastern wing.

Evangeline. Thank heavens.

The temptation to make his way immediately over to her was there, but his military training was stronger. You didn't move out into an open area unless you were completely certain that it was safe.

He wet his fingers and put them to his lips, letting out a sharp whistle before darting back into the trees. Evangeline's head shot up. She looked quickly around then hurried over.

She passed right by where Gus stood, continuing on to the next cluster of trees.

Good girl. You know how to make sure no one has followed.

Slipping out from his secret spot, he crept around to the other side of where Evangeline hid. A glimpse of her chocolate brown hair was all he got before she launched herself at him.

"*Dieu merci. Dieu merci,*" she said, wrapping her arms around him tightly.

Gus winced. "*Un peu plus léger, s'il vous plaît?*"

She froze, then released her hold on him entirely. "Oh, I am so sorry. I forgot you had been shot. Forgive me. How is your wound?"

He smiled at her. "I am mostly recovered; and Evangeline, you are always forgiven. I just wish I could have come back sooner. I cannot begin to tell you the nightmares I have endured worrying about you."

She lay a hand on his chest, right over the wound. "It is a miracle that you survived. I know I told you not to come, but I would be lying if I said I wasn't relieved to see you."

I could never stay away, not when I thought you might be in danger.

He placed his hand over hers, brushing his thumb gently back and forth. Their gazes met for a brief moment before she slipped her hand free and stepped back. Her behavior had Gus pondering Evangeline's reasons for having made such a bold move. And also, as to why he had stroked her hand.

We haven't been this way with one another before. Is it just because I almost died? Or is it something else?

Gus pushed those awkward questions to the back of his mind. He was here on a mission, and that had to come first. "How are things? Are they as bad as your note said?"

Evangeline nodded. "Worse. Vincent Marec is demanding that Armand hand over the entire smuggling operation to him. He also wants us out of the château. That man will take everything we have if given the chance."

"And what of Armand? Is he still preparing to fight?"

She lifted her gaze to the heavens and let out a resigned sigh. "He is determined to fight to the bitter end. He has enough weapons to start a small war, but he is no soldier. Vincent has years of military experience to call upon, and he won't ever concede defeat."

"This doesn't make sense; Armand has never been one for violence."

"I know. His moods are constantly shifting. One minute he is the Armand I have known all my life—warm, loving, a true bon vivant. The next he is sharpening blades."

"Well, I am here now. I will talk to your uncle and get him to see reason." Gus stepped away in the direction of the path, and Evangeline followed. The sooner he confronted Armand the better.

※

She had never been so relieved to see another person in her entire life. The instant she had heard Gus's whistle, hope flared in Evangeline's heart. He had come. And with him, the chance that a rational, sane man might finally be able talk Armand out of his secret plan. To bring her uncle back to sanity.

"Where is Armand now?"

"He has gone into Saint-Brieuc. He wouldn't tell me why. Armand has become quite secretive of late, not willing to share anything. All he does is walk around the house muttering to himself. And he has put new locks on several doors in the west wing and won't let me have the keys."

She wasn't even welcome in his study anymore; a place where she had shared many happy hours with her uncle. The previous evening, she had walked in on Armand while he was seated at his desk. She had caught sight of what looked like plans for a cannon before harsh words had been exchanged. He had thrown her out and locked the door.

Evangeline's gaze met Gus's deep brown eyes. He was wearing his customary tricorne hat and false long-haired wig. His smugglers disguise.

While it was charming, the hat also partially hid Gus's face. She hoped that one day, she might be able to convince him to move with the times and wear the more fashionable top hat.

And perhaps give up the wig.

She understood all too well that the hat, greatcoat, and wig were all part of his attempt to blend in with the local Breton population, but she would dearly love to see more of the real Gus. The man beneath the façade.

If only you would let down your guard. You might even see me standing right in front of you.

He cleared his throat, and the spell was broken. "I need to go and inform the captain and crew of my yacht that I am safe. If I don't, they will think something has happened and sail on to Binic."

"Why would they do that? What is at Binic?"

The seaport of Binic was some eight miles farther west along the coast. It was a pretty fishing village, but she couldn't understand why they would move the yacht there.

"The men who sailed with me last night were not exactly leaping up and down with joy at the news of making this trip. I had to make certain undertakings about their protection in order to get them to come. Because it is far enough away from here, Binic offers a degree of safety for both them and the boat," he replied.

His words pulled her up sharp. Few of his crew had been willing to make the trip.

So much for reinforcements.

"Did you bring any of the other members of the RR Coaching Company with you?" she ventured.

She had been hoping that Sir Stephen Moore or at least George Hawkins would be waiting on board the *Night Wind*. The more of the rogues of the road she could press into service, the better. They were men her uncle trusted. People he might actually be inclined to listen to, and who could stop him from launching into whatever crazy scheme he had in mind.

Gus shook his head. "Just me I am afraid. Stephen's wife, Bridget, is with child, and she has already been widowed once. George's wife would nail his foot to the floor if he so much as took a step in the direction of France. Harry's wife is due to deliver their first child any day. And Monsale has a date with Madame Guillotine if he ever dares to set foot in this country again."

"Which leaves only you." There was no point in trying to hide her disappointment—it was evident in her voice. She had prayed for an army and got one soldier. Gus was a warrior, but he couldn't fight the whole of Vincent's army on his own.

Gus glanced at the path which led down the hill and back to the jetty. "Let me go and speak to Captain Grey. I won't be long."

As he walked away, Evangeline chided herself. "He has risked his life in coming here, and you greeted him with scant regard."

After such a poor reward for his efforts, she wouldn't be the least surprised if Gus got back on his boat and returned to England. She wasn't worthy of his bravery.

Chapter Six

After spending a good half-hour arguing with the crew of the *Night Wind* as to whether it was prudent or not for them to venture into Saint-Brieuc and pay their respects to the women of the local taverns, a frustrated Gus headed back up the hill.

"What happened to being afraid for your lives? Too busy thinking with your cocks and not your heads," he grumbled.

His temper was further stretched to its limits when he returned to the château. Armand La Roche had still not returned. There was little Gus could do until he had spoken to the man.

Evangeline was wrapped up in a thick woolen shawl as she stepped out of the main house. Gus who had been about to enter the foyer, moved to one side to let her pass.

"When do you expect Armand to return?" he asked.

Evangeline shrugged her shoulders. "I don't know. As I have explained, he doesn't tell me anything anymore. There are men coming and going in the courtyard all the time. Carts delivering crates at odd hours of the day."

He nodded at her shawl. "Where are you off to?"

"For a walk. I need some sea air to clear my head," she replied, fatigue evident in her voice.

He was tempted to go back to the boat, then thought better of the idea. "Let me come with you."

Evangeline marched all the way to the center of the courtyard then turned to face the house. A bemused Gus followed suit.

Château-de-La-Roche wasn't a grand structure such as the magnificent châteaux of the Loire valley, instead it was closer in architectural design to a large English manor house. Some twenty or so rooms were shared over three levels. He appreciated its simple design.

The eastern wing of the château had been constructed at a ninety-degree angle to the western side, with the spiked turret at the intersection of the two wings. It was a clever piece of architecture, which afforded protection to the courtyard from the strong winds which blew in from the English Channel.

Evangeline pointed to the metal griffin perched high on the top of the spike, where it acted as a weathervane. "Did you know that my late father once climbed all the way up there in the middle of a storm? The servants were too frightened, but he was determined to stop the griffin from falling."

She spun on her heel and pointed in the direction of the kitchen garden.

"After the revolutionary committee for the protection of the French Republic took this place from us, we were made to go and live in a tiny cottage in Saint-Brieuc. When they finally abandoned this place, and we were allowed to return, my mother and I spent endless hours restoring the herb garden."

Gus waited; Evangeline was building up to something big.

Tears glistened in her eyes, and there was a tremble in her voice. "We were only gone for four years. In that time, the various citizens committees for the revolution, which had use of this place, abused it most horribly. They did everything but destroy it. And now . . ."

She waved a hand in the air.

"Now Marec and his bandits want to take it from us again. My family were good to the people of this area. We still are, and this is the reward we get?"

Her head dropped at the same time as her arm. "I am sorry, Gus; I am glad you came. It's just that I was hoping for more. Armand likes you, and that is a particular problem. Sir Stephen has always been firm with my uncle, and he listens to him."

And he may not pay heed to what I have to say.

Gus scrunched his lips together, fighting to keep his temper under control. He had every right to be offended by Evangeline's words. She had basically just told him he was useless.

But getting angry wouldn't solve anything. It would only serve to fracture the fragile bond between them. He wanted nothing more than to come to her, to offer reassurances and comfort.

He might not be able to reach Armand, but he understood Evangeline and how her mind worked. A soft pat on the arm and a kind word was not the way to deal with her. A change in tack was required. "You said in your letter that your uncle wouldn't listen to you, that he is determined to fight Marec. So, why do you think he would pay heed to anyone? To be frank, I am not here to stop him from going to war."

Her brows lifted.

You weren't expecting to hear that.

"Why are you here then?"

He took a step closer. "To do what I can to support Armand, but also to help you. If things go as badly as I expect they might, you are going to need me. Evangeline, I came to France for you."

Heat raced to Evangeline's cheeks. When Gus took another step closer, she wanted nothing more than to flee. Roguish Englishmen were dangerous. She had long held that opinion from her dealings with the members of the rogues of the road. Augustus Jones in particular had always set her nerves inexplicably on edge.

He had come to France for her. Evangeline struggled to understand what that really meant. She had written to Gus because she was concerned about Armand. Her uncle's life was in danger. Saving him and the family home were what mattered.

I have to get away.

"I must go and check with the kitchen. Make sure the plans for the roast perch and fennel supper are progressing. Armand will be in need of a good meal when he returns. Excuse me." She made for the garden gate but didn't go back inside the main house. Instead, she moved quickly past the vegetable beds, deftly sidestepped a wandering chicken, and then headed straight toward the path which led down to the sea chapel.

Her blood was pounding hard in her ears, but it was not loud enough to cover the sound of Gus's boots.

"Evangeline, wait," he said.

"No."

She kept up her hurried pace, only finally slowing when she reached the stone steps. They were old and worn. Only a fool would try to descend them at any sort of speed.

Fifty-three steps. The last half-dozen or so were wet and slippery from the sea mist, slowing her progress even further. Gus caught up with her as she put her foot on the last one.

He took a firm hold of her arm and helped her down.

"You can't run away from me. Where will you go?" he pleaded.

She turned to face him. "You said you came for me. But what about Armand? I am afraid for him. Not just what Vincent and his men will do, but what my uncle is scheming. Gus, I fear it is something big, and once he lets it loose, no one will be able to control it, least of all him."

He released his hold and followed her into the chapel.

The moment she stepped inside, everything changed. Light and sounds from the world disappeared, replaced by the sense of being somewhere that was almost ethereal. Nothing could compare to how standing in the tiny cave made her feel.

On the far side of it the blue sea which lay beyond could be seen through a small gap in the rock face. The waves, dancing up and down, captured in a living frame.

Suspended from the roof of the sea chapel was a small silver bell, rarely rung these days. On the near wall, behind a stone altar, was a rack for votive candles. Evangeline took in the rows of fallen, burned-out beeswax. This place had become forgotten. Lost.

It was sad that no one, apart from her, came here. Even she rarely did these days. Life was too busy. Too many pressing conflicts for her time to indulge in precious moments of quiet reflection.

She closed her eyes as the cool sea salt air kissed her face. If she had to choose a place on earth to spend her last minutes of existence, it would be here.

Gus came to her side, slipping his hat from his head. "I had forgotten about this place. It is magical."

Opening her eyes, she turned to him. Her gaze fell on his face. On those warm brown eyes. Gus wasn't a handsome man in the traditional sense of the word. His charm lay beyond such mundane things as appearances.

"Forgive me, Gus. I am grateful that you are here. And I think you are right. Talking won't likely get you anywhere with my uncle. I would be grateful if you could do what you can to help him, but please don't put yourself in danger. None of this is worth it."

He slipped an arm around her shoulder. "This is your home. No one has the right to take it from you. Your family has protected this holy chapel for many years. Men like Vincent Marec don't deserve to set foot in here."

"No, but he will. I can feel it in my bones. We are going to lose this place."

There was nothing Evangeline could do to stop the inevitable. She could only pray that somewhere within the ranks of Marec's followers was a man capable of understanding the precious beauty of the chapel. Someone who would become its new guardian.

She lay her head against Gus's chest, relieved that at least some things hadn't changed. He had answered her prayers and come to France. "I have missed you, Augustus Trajan Jones. I spent many hours here after you had left, praying that you would live."

That you would come back.

"I survived because people like you and Stephen cared. And because Captain Grey is handy with a heated knife."

He pointed to the simple gold cross which sat on the altar. "And I believe I was spared so that I could return here. I can't quite put it into words, but I have a feeling that my task here is more than just about dealing with the problem of Vincent Marec."

Chapter Seven

After leaving the chapel, they made their way down to the sandy beach of the nearby cove. It was a small area, only big enough to bring a small rowboat ashore, hence the need to build the jetty in the river on the other side of the hill.

The walk from the chapel gave Evangeline precious time in which to muster her bravery. She stepped onto the sand and faced the sea, too scared to look at Gus who followed close behind. "What did you mean when you said you came back to France for me?"

A hard male body pressed against her back. She closed her eyes as her imagination took over. Many nights she had lain awake in her bed and thought of Gus. Of what being with him would be like.

"I spent weeks recuperating at Monsale House. The Duke of Monsale is not one for idle chatter, so there were many hours when I was alone. During that time, I thought about you. Of what I might have missed had that bullet pierced my heart."

"And what did you think you would have missed?"

Strong arms spun her around to face him.

His hands were placed either side of her face, and he

leaned in. Her gaze settled on his lips. On the soft smile which sat on them.

"This."

Gus pressed his lips to hers. His kiss was tentative at first, and she sensed he was waiting for her response. To see whether he had read her wrong.

He hadn't.

Her lips parted, and Gus deepened the kiss. Their tongues met and danced over one another in strong, passionate strokes.

Everything else in the world disappeared. It was just the two of them. Even the noise of the crashing waves on the nearby rocks fell to a dim, almost imperceptible whisper.

When Gus speared his fingers through her hair, Evangeline silently congratulated herself for her impetuous ways. Braids be damned, this was how a woman wanted a man to hold her as he kissed her senseless.

He really has come for me.

Chapter Eight

It was close on midnight before Armand finally returned to Château-de-La-Roche. While he was polite with his greetings, Gus was immediately struck by the evasive and strange way his friend behaved. Evangeline bore the brunt of her uncle's temper.

Armand pointed a finger angrily at her. "Did you ask him to come here to undermine me? Is that it? You think me a simpleton unable to defend my own home?"

"No. I just thought he could help. He is a friend," she replied.

"You seek to betray me. Just like Marec and his men. Get out of my sight."

Gus stood stunned. This was not the Armand La Roche he had known for many years. The man who had laughed as he helped to row brandy out to the *Night Wind* in the middle of a raging storm when it was too dangerous to attempt to come up the Gouët river.

A tearful and chastised Evangeline quickly fled the room, closing the door loudly behind her.

Armand huffed, raking his fingers through his salt and pepper flecked hair.

"Armand, she . . ."

"I know." He held up a hand, stopping Gus from finishing what he was about to say.

The angry, manic expression disappeared from Armand's face, replaced by something close to sadness. "I didn't want you to come to France because I need somewhere to send Evangeline. My plan was to put her on a boat to England. To send her to you."

You could have knocked Gus down with a feather. This was not anything he had ever considered. "But you could send her to Paris. To your son, Louis."

Armand shook his head. "Paris is a long way from here. She would never make it that far. Marec is a more determined and dangerous man that you realize. He and Evangeline were friends once. But she has crossed him one too many times. If I lose the war against him, he will come for her."

Come for her?

That could mean a number of different things, all of which Gus feared.

"What are you not telling me?" he replied.

"Marec has threatened me with exposure to the authorities in Paris. If I don't hand the château over to him, he says he will bring charges of sedition and consorting with the enemy against me."

France and England had still been at war when the rogues of the road and Armand had first struck up their bargain to move contraband between the two countries. The money-making enterprise could be seen by some as treason. The penalty for those found guilty, death.

Many people on both sides of the English Channel had been involved in smuggling goods during the long hostilities. All knew the risk they were taking. A shilling here, a franc there had kept palms greased and lips shut. But there was always the chance of betrayal.

Armand will kill himself rather than be arrested.

"Marec wants me to break any agreements that you and I have. He will forge new ones with his other partners. We are to be cut out of the smuggling trade along this part of the coast."

The news of Marec pushing to take over the operations was of little surprise to Gus. The past year had seen many new players enter the smuggling business; things were getting crowded. Trade was still lucrative for those who could manage the means of supply and distribution. The RR Coaching Company and the La Roche family ran a reliable operation.

"Well, that's what Marec thinks is going to happen. I sent word offering to meet with him here later this week. The arrogant fool will probably expect me just to hand over the keys to my home and stroll out the front door. He is going to be in for a nasty surprise," snorted Armand.

Gus finally got his first glimpse of what Evangeline had been talking about. Armand was up to something big, and he didn't want anyone else knowing about his plans.

He narrowed his eyes at the Frenchman. He was determined to get answers. "What are you planning? It is bad enough that you are hurting Evangeline in the name of keeping her safe. But, Armand, you can't do that with me."

What he really wanted to say was that Evangeline was not a little girl and shouldn't be kept in the dark, but an argument with his old friend wouldn't solve anything.

"Please. Let me help you."

Armand scrubbed at his face with his hands. He oozed fear and irritability. From the bags under his eyes, Gus hazarded a guess that the Frenchman had not seen a decent night's sleep in quite some time.

"Thank you, my friend, but this is my war not yours. You shouldn't have to risk your life for me."

"I want to help."

"Alright," Armand sighed. "I am to meet with Marec later

in the week. Perhaps he might have second thoughts if you are standing alongside me. In the meantime, you can be of use. If you could take the *Night Wind* up the coast to Binic and pick up a shipment of brandy tomorrow, I would be most grateful. Marec has made things difficult dealing directly with the merchants in Lamballe, so I have had to make some changes. Do you know Binic?"

"I have sailed past it many times. It's only a short way up the coast from Saint-Brieuc."

Armand gave the merest of nods.

Gus wasn't going to make mention that not only did he know the village of Binic well, having slipped ashore there a number of times during the war, but that he and Captain Grey had already agreed to send the *Night Wind* there if things went awry in the fight against Vincent Marec and his men.

Being unsure as to whether he could trust Armand at this point, Gus decided it was better to keep any contingency plans a secret. "Alright. I shall take the yacht up to Binic. We should talk about Evangeline when I get back."

"Agreed. She needs to be somewhere safe. And the best place would be with you, in England…as your wife."

Chapter Nine

The bruises and bags under Gus's eyes were nothing like those of Armand, but they were enough to let anyone who looked closely know that he had not had much sleep.

The Frenchman's first request was an easy enough task. The *Night Wind* headed back out into the English Channel the following morning, bound for Binic. A short sail to collect the crates of brandy and then return to the château.

It was Armand's second that had kept Gus awake and staring out into the night. At one point, he had got out of bed, dressed, and made his way down to the sea chapel. He wasn't a religious man by nature, but the peace and solitude of the cool, limestone cave brought his worried mind some respite. His thoughts the whole time had been of Evangeline.

Marriage hadn't been in his plans, at least not yet. He was still struggling with his own feelings toward Evangeline, of what they might mean.

The kiss at the beach had been an impulsive act on his part. One minute he was trying to think of how he could offer her support, the next he was hauling her into his arms.

I am attracted to her, but marriage has to be based on more than mere lust.

Standing on the deck of the *Night Wind* watching as the coastline of Brittany drifted by on the portside, he went back to pondering what he was to do.

He and Evangeline had shared a kiss, but was that enough? Marriage wasn't just a passing fancy; it was a life-long commitment. Asking her to suddenly uproot her life and move to England couldn't just be based on the first blush of a romance.

She would not take kindly to being forced into marriage. Especially not to someone like me. A smuggler. A rogue. An Englishman.

Evangeline was a willful, strong-minded woman. Not one taken to accepting direction or instruction easily.

She would not be tamed.

Nor should she. This is a woman, not a wild thing to tie up and break. Her fiery nature is part of who she is. If you try to change her, you will only crush her soul.

Evangeline La Roche would need to be treated with careful respect. Her intelligence not only acknowledged but accepted. Marriage would have to be a true partnership.

"She will fight tooth and nail to stay here in France. To remain by her uncle's side," he muttered.

Evangeline could wield a rifle better than most men. Another good reason for Armand to want her far away. She wouldn't hold back if it came to a gunfight.

Whichever way things went with the Lamballe gang, he was going to have to tread carefully when it came to Evangeline.

I need to get her away from the château and somewhere safe. Distance will help with perspective.

"She has to have other options if things go awry."

They both did.

He was still musing over the problem of what to do about Evangeline and her uncle when the *Night Wind* docked in the small fishing village of Binic. Gus and his friends had used it as a secret base during the war, so he knew the place well. The rogues of the road still maintained a safe house in Rue Martin.

This morning's destination was a tall, narrow warehouse situated at the far end of the waterfront. The nondescript gray stone building was well out of the way. The plain, faded sign which read *Poissonnier* belied the real use of the premises, as a front for Armand's smuggling operations. Gus suspected the place hadn't operated as a fishmonger for many years.

While the crew busied themselves with collecting crates and carrying them the short distance back to the *Night Wind*, Gus approached Armand's Binic connection.

The man clearly hadn't been expecting a boatload of Englishmen to arrive and take the brandy. He was almost as evasive as his employer. "The bottles should have been moved by cart. The sea might be too rough for them," he said.

Gus frowned. He had been transporting crates of brandy bottles on board his ship for as long as he could remember. He couldn't recall a single bottle ever having been spoiled. "My men are quite experienced at handling this sort of cargo. Armand trusts me," he replied.

He shouldn't be having to explain himself, but the man's demeanor had Gus worried. He led him away from where the *Night Wind* crew were working.

"My friend. You appear worried. Please, share your concerns," he said.

The store man met his gaze. It was clear he was studying Gus, deciding whether he was someone trustworthy. "Have you checked any of the bottles? I mean closely," he asked.

Trust between smugglers was a golden rule. Unlike pirates, it was expected that you took a man at his word. Opening crates and checking the cargo was tantamount to calling a man a liar and a thief. And while smugglers were clearly both these things, you just didn't remind them of that fact. Not unless you wanted to have a short career in the business, followed by a long swim in the sea.

There was something in his tone which set Gus's nerves on edge. "No. Should I?"

He was handed a bottle of brandy. Or at least what should have been brandy. Instead of the usual golden liquid floating inside, it was black.

"Is that?" he asked.

"Yes. Gunpowder. All the crates are full of it. Armand hasn't taken any brandy from the warehouse in the past month. What we have been doing, however, is filling bottles with powder and sending it by cart over land."

"How many loads have you sent?"

"At least five. I am not happy with having that much explosive stored here. It's too dangerous. I dread to think where Armand is keeping it at the château."

And what he intends to do with it.

"Thank you for telling me this, *mon ami*. It could well save lives."

Captain Grey appeared at the door of the building and approached. A worried look sat on his face. "We have a problem," he said.

Gus looked from the captain to the store man. "Are you referring to the contents of the bottles?"

Captain Grey nodded. "Gunpowder. The crew complained about how heavy the crates were in comparison to the usual ones. I know I was breaking the code, but I decided to take a look."

Gus wasn't going to chastise the yacht's captain. He might be the *Night Wind's* owner, but while it was at sea, Captain Grey was the man calling the shots. He was well within his rights to make sure nothing noxious or dangerous was on board.

"Apparently Armand has been collecting bottles of gunpowder for some time," replied Gus.

The question which now sat front and center of his mind —why would Armand be moving gunpowder in such a way? Small bottles would take time to empty, and then the powder would have to be stored once more.

But what if he wasn't taking it out of the bottles . . . Oh merde!

They had just picked up a shipment of ready-made explosives.

He had to find out where the rest of the gunpowder was being stored at the château. If Armand was foolish enough to be hiding it in the main house, behind locked doors, then Château-de-La-Roche could be sitting right on top of an unexploded bomb. One of monumental proportions.

Something else suddenly dropped into his thoughts, and Gus turned to the store man. "So, what you are saying is that Armand has never sent any of this cargo by sea before today?"

"Yes. That is why I thought it strange that you suddenly arrived this morning."

We weren't expected. Which means we didn't need to go up the coast to Binic today. Not unless Armand wanted me out of the way. Oh no.

Gus's blood turned to ice. He would bet a thousand francs that Vincent Marec and Armand were meeting today. The final confrontation taking place while he was conveniently out of the way.

"Tell the crew to abandon loading the boat. We have to get back to the château as fast as possible."

Armand, you fool, you wanted to keep Evangeline safe, but your pride will get her killed.

Chapter Ten

✦

One of the estate laborers came racing at breakneck speed into the kitchen of Château-de-La-Roche. Baskets of fresh fruits and vegetables went flying.

"Marec and his men are coming up the road from the valley. They are carrying lances and guns!" he cried.

The wheel of cheese Evangeline had been holding dropped with a thud onto the table, and she bolted for the door. Running around to the front of the château, she came to a skittering halt. There was a heavily armed horde bearing down on her family home.

Vincent Marec, mounted on his black steed, rode at the head of a small army. He looked for all the world like a general come to sack and plunder. This was not the usual small gang of villains he had in his employ. This was an invasion.

For a moment, she stood rooted to the spot, unable to move.

"*Que le ciel nous aide,*" she whispered.

But she was no fool. They would need more than just a touch of divine intervention if they were going to beat back this threat. Tears pricked at her eyes. The day had finally come.

She turned to the group of servants who had gathered behind her. "Get everyone out of the château. Clear the grounds. Save yourselves. Go!"

The estate staff scattered in all directions, leaving Evangeline alone.

"At least Gus is up the coast and away from all this insanity," she muttered.

By the time the *Night Wind* returned, it would likely be all over. If he was here, they would surely kill him. An Englishman against an army of former French soldiers wouldn't stand a chance. His would be a senseless death.

Picking up her skirts, she sprinted for the front door of the château. "Uncle! Armand! They are coming!"

She frantically searched for him. Armand was nowhere to be seen. Then her gaze settled on the door to the formal dining room. Her uncle had been keeping it locked of late, with no one allowed to go inside.

With a racing heart, she tried the handle. It pushed open. She stopped, taken aback by the odd sight of dozens of crates stacked all the way to the ceiling. They had never stored brandy inside the house.

Armand turned as she entered the room. "Is Marec here?" he asked.

He knew the Lamballe gang were coming.

"Yes, he has brought an army."

Armand swore. "He said he would come alone today. That man is a liar. I should have known he would prove false."

Evangeline stared at the crates, trying to make sense of them. If they had all this brandy, why had Armand sent Gus to Binic to pick up more?

Armand met her gaze, then glanced back at the crates. "I know what you are thinking. But the contents of those crates are not brandy. It's gunpowder."

He sent Gus to Binic because he wanted him out of the way when Marec got here. None of this makes sense.

There was one thing Evangeline did know for certain, and that was that Vincent Marec wasn't here to negotiate. He was coming to seize their home.

"We have to leave, Uncle. We cannot fight them," she said.

"No and yes," he replied.

"What?"

"No, I am not leaving, and yes, there is little point in fighting them. I was hoping it wouldn't come to this, but now it seems a change of plans is in order."

She recognized the Armand of old as he took a hold of her hand and raised it to his lips. "My dear Evangeline. You are such a brave girl. A credit to our family. It falls to me to do everything I can to stop that evil brute from getting his hands on you. Which means that I need you to do exactly as I say. Please?"

"But Uncle . . . Yes, of course."

"Go upstairs this instant and pack just enough things to fit in a saddlebag. Make sure you get your rifle. Then go to my private study—the door is not locked. Take out the cloth pouch which is in the top drawer of my desk. I feared there might be trouble, so I instructed the horse master to have Gobain saddled and waiting for you in the stables."

Evangeline had long feared this day would come, but now that it was here, her nerve faltered. She wasn't nearly as brave as she had thought she was.

"We are all servants of a higher power. You have your role to play, as do I. Now go, before it is too late. I will not have you die—or worse, today."

Fighting back a rising tide of panic and fear, Evangeline forced herself to do as Armand instructed. In her room, she gathered a couple of sensible woolen gowns and stuffed them into a leather satchel. Dressed in her late father's greatcoat and with her rifle in hand, she made her way to Armand's study.

Inside the top drawer, she found the money pouch. She gasped when she opened it and saw the coins inside. It was a substantial sum. More than enough for her to make it safely to one of the nearby major cities.

More than enough to start over somewhere.

Armand was sending her out into the world on her own.

She startled at the loud bang which echoed up the stairs. Someone had just kicked open the front door. There was yelling and cries of pain and outrage from the servants as they were bustled outside.

"Evangeline La Roche, come to me, or I will drag you headfirst down the stairs!" bellowed Vincent.

With her heart thumping hard, she made her way downstairs. Her hopes of remaining at her home dying instantly at the sight which greeted her.

Vincent stood in the middle of the room; legs spread wide, full of obvious self-importance. In his hand he held a flaming torch.

Behind Vincent was Claude, the scar-faced man whose hat Evangeline had put a bullet through a few weeks earlier.

Have they come to burn the place down? I thought they wanted the château.

Vincent turned from glowering at Armand. "Ah, there you are dear, sweet Evangeline."

Evangeline came and stood alongside Armand. She dropped her gaze to her feet, not wishing to tempt fate. Vincent Marec was a man with an unpredictable and explosive temper. If there was any chance of her and Armand getting out of the château alive, she was going to have to play it smart and adopt the role of defeated, docile female. "Vincent," she said.

The crunch of his heavy boots echoed on the stone floor.

She kept her gaze downward. Hard, cruel fingers seized her chin, and her head was thrust violently upward.

She met a pair of cold, gray eyes. They had always reminded her of the sea when a dark and wicked storm was about to hit.

He nodded at the satchel on her back. "At least you have packed, unlike Armand," he sniffed.

"I don't want to leave my home," she said, addressing her uncle.

Armand nodded. "I know, but the battle is lost. We must do what we can." He bowed to Vincent. "Would you please give me a few minutes to put some things in a bag? And then let me say a quick, final goodbye to my home."

Vincent looked from Armand to Evangeline. "Alright, but she stays here with me. Or better still, Evangeline, you could go out to the stables. When we arrived, I noticed Gobain was saddled and ready to leave. How convenient. Claude can accompany you. I am sure he has a few choice words he would like to share about what he thinks of you having shot him."

The villain in question grinned at her, licking his lips as his gaze settled on her breasts.

Fiend. Just try it and see how well life goes for you without your manhood.

Evangeline glanced at her rifle. "I didn't shoot you, monsieur. As I recall it was your hat which received the bullet. Perhaps I should be apologizing to it."

Vincent snapped his fingers. "Enough. Take her outside. And Claude, if you are foolish enough to try anything else, Evangeline has my full permission to shoot you properly this time. No one touches what belongs to me."

I will never be yours. I would rather die.

As she was dragged toward the front door, Evangeline caught a final glimpse of Armand as he headed toward the stairs. Vincent, meanwhile, prowled about the ground floor, brandishing the flaming torch.

There was an awful lot of gunpowder stored in the château. The prospect of a naked flame only a matter of feet away from what was tantamount to a powder keg had Evangeline praying that Armand wouldn't spend too long saying his farewells to their home.

The sooner they were far away from Château-de-La-Roche the better.

Thank God he sent Gus up the coast. If Armand doesn't do anything rash, we might yet escape with our lives.

Chapter Eleven

Claude—Evangeline had never bothered to inquire as to his surname—was a short man, gruff in nature. He huffed and panted all the way from the front door of the château to the stables. He appeared to be struggling with his breathing.

Once inside the stables, he loosened his hold on Evangeline then roughly shoved her away. He pointed at her rifle. "Don't even think about it. Besides, I wouldn't be tempted by Vincent's whore."

She winced at the callous remark. A woman made one mistake in her life and she was forever branded as being fallen.

And yet, you have probably lain with dozens of women, but you don't see me judging you for it.

He stopped for a moment and doubled over. His hands rested on his knees as he wheezed and coughed. The strain showed on his quickly reddening face. Evangeline found herself unintentionally trying to breathe for him.

Finally, he righted himself and swallowed deeply. "Exploding cannon, at the Battle of Corunna in '09. I was fighting the English while your family were finding ways to work with them." The tone of disapproval and disgust in his voice was unmistakable.

"I know you probably couldn't care less, but my family didn't get involved in smuggling until after the committee for the revolution ransacked this place. And then it was only after Napoleon had been sent to Elba. The war was nearly over."

He snorted. "You are right. I couldn't give a damn about your family. Get your horse."

A subdued Evangeline walked to where Gobain, her beloved horse stood. If she could keep the magnificent bay, it would be an unexpected blessing. She slung the satchel containing all her earthly possessions over her shoulder and aimed her foot at the stirrup.

The whole world erupted.

An almighty explosion ripped through the air. The wind was punched out of her lungs as she hit the hard stone floor of the stables. Gobain reared up, screaming with fright.

For a moment, she lay stunned. It took all her effort to simply breathe. A loud ringing filled her ears.

What just happened?

Rolling over onto her knees, Evangeline could make out the figure of Claude flat on his back. She staggered to her feet and tottered over to where Vincent's man lay still. His eyes were closed, but to her relief, his chest rose and fell. He had been knocked out cold.

A second massive explosion tore through the air, throwing her once more to the ground. Then a series of smaller blasts quickly followed. *Boom. Boom. Boom.*

Footsteps pounded outside as people scattered in all directions, crying and wailing in terror.

"Armand," she whispered.

Her horse dashed itself against the wooden side of the stalls, struggling to break free. If she didn't come to his aid, Gobain would surely harm himself.

Blinking hard, fighting against the roar in her ears, Evangeline made her way over to the frightened animal. After taking a hold of the bridle, she pulled down hard, doing her best to steady him. She patted the side of his head and gently soothed. "It's alright, Gobain. I shall get you out of here."

It took several minutes before the horse finally settled, and she was safely able to untie the reins. After carefully leading Gobain out to the front of the stables, she came to a halt.

Fear made her wish not to look, but there was no escape. What had once been the west wing of the château was now a smoking ruin. Flames shot high into the gray afternoon sky. The whole roof had collapsed in on itself.

Smoke poured out of every window. Even the griffin on the top of the weathervane was clouded in a gust of floating black ash.

Destruction was everywhere.

The front door of the château crashed open, and Vincent staggered out. He dropped to his knees, coughing and spluttering.

Evangeline reached for her rifle, cursing when she realized it was still in the stables. If she'd had it at hand, she wouldn't have hesitated to shoot him.

"Armand!" she screamed.

She took two steps forward then stopped as three of the Lamballe gang rushed over to Vincent and lifted their stricken leader. They carried him over to his horse, and with some effort managed to get him in the saddle. He took a hold of the reins but remained motionless, head bowed. Finally, one of his men gave a hard slap to the beast's rump, and it jumped away, tearing down the road at great speed.

There was a sickening screech, followed by yet another loud crash. Evangeline whirled round as the tall spire of the center turret collapsed and fell. The intense heat from the fire had melted it. The La Roche family griffin crashed to earth in the courtyard.

The flames continued to burn on in the château, consuming everything in their wake.

Thank god the servants all got out before the château blew.

For what seemed like an eternity, Evangeline stood staring at the front door of the house, willing Armand to appear from out of the thick, black smoke. She would give anything for a miracle.

You wanted a war, Uncle, but not like this. You never stood a chance against such villainy. How could Vincent set the flame to our home? Why?

Her hands slowly clenched tightly into fists. The need for vengeance now burning as hot as the flames which continued to consume the château. Vincent may well have managed to survive the explosion, but he was far from out of danger.

He was now a marked man. Evangeline would have her revenge for the death of her beloved Armand. She headed back into the stables to fetch her rifle.

A few minutes later, saddlebags filled with gunpowder and shot, Gobain galloped at full speed out of the stables and toward the front gate. On his back, Evangeline lay low over the reins.

The Lamballe gang had fired the first volley in this battle, but while they limped away intending to go home and nurse their wounds, she was hot on their trail. Evangeline La Roche was going to rain the fire and fury of vengeance down upon them.

Chapter Twelve

❦

The acrid smell of smoke drifted to Gus's nose not long after the *Night Wind* sailed into the mouth of the Gouët river. He glanced up at the medieval ruins of the Cesson tower which overlooked where the bay of Saint-Brieuc and the Gouët met.

He sniffed at the air. It wasn't uncommon for the locals to set fire to parts of the overgrown woodland around the base of the tower in order to clear land for their livestock. But the odor which sat on the wind was not one of burning trees or grass.

"The château is ablaze!"

Gus turned his gaze to where the member of his crew was pointing. A thick, black plume of smoke filled the sky above where Château-de-La-Roche stood. The sickening boom of explosions reached his ears.

"I hope that is not anywhere near where Armand has hidden the gunpowder," he muttered.

Brandy was bad enough, but if the flames got into the powder store, the whole place could go up. And if it did, anyone within a hundred yards would be in peril.

Evangeline. Where in the middle of all this are you?

A horrid, sinking feeling settled over him. Knowing Evangeline La Roche, she would be right in the thick of fighting the blaze. She would be tossing buckets of water on the flames with no regard for her own safety.

"Sails. I want every sail aloft!" he bellowed.

For a moment, he was tempted to leap overboard and swim to shore, but the yacht was still too far from land.

Captain Grey came to his side. "We have every sail in the wind. I cannot bring the boat in any faster. And besides . . ."

An anxious Gus glared at him. He never liked it when the captain added a *besides* to his comments.

"What?"

The other man sighed. "The last time you went racing up the path to the château, you returned with a bullet wound and I had to cut it out of your chest. Or have you forgotten the long night you endured on the way back to England?"

Gus would never forget that night. "I won't go dashing into anything. If the château is under attack, I would be a fool to blindly step right in the middle of it."

And he had made a promise to his father not to die a hero.

The captain nodded his agreement as the crew of the *Night Wind* scrambled around the weather deck, shifting canvas about in the wind as fast as they could.

Gus stayed well clear. He was a good sailor, but in this sort of situation he would only impede their work. His injured left shoulder made him more of a hindrance than any help.

It was a tense few minutes before the boat finally drew up alongside the quay. As several of the crew, ropes in hand, made ready to jump over the side and moor the yacht, Gus considered where he was best to head once he set foot on dry land.

From the riverside it was obvious the château was well alight. Nothing and no one could save it.

His hand had just settled on the top of the gunwale when

a sickening boom reverberated through the air. The sky above was suddenly full of burning wood, splinters, and stones; they rained down upon the crew. Everyone on board the boat ducked for cover, but several men were hit by flying debris.

Staggering to his feet, Gus took in the disaster. The water around the jetty was full of floating flotsam and jetsam. Injured crew members sat bloodied on the deck. The truth of Armand's reckless plans lay in front of him.

Oh Armand, why store it in the house?

Gus squinted, straining to see, but the gray cloud of dust and smoke which enveloped the area surrounding the château was impenetrable. A hand on his arm had him meeting the worried face of the yacht's captain. "Mister Jones, you aren't going ashore, are you? Who is to say that the last of it went up in that explosion? There might be more gunpowder still ready to blow."

Gus nodded. "I hear you, but I have to go. My friends. I must find out what has happened to them. Stay here and render whatever assistance you can to the crew. Then you need to sail clear. I won't have these men dying today."

"But what about you?"

"Don't worry about me. Get the boat away. We have all those crates of gunpowder on the deck and below. The last place the *Night Wind* should be is anywhere near fire. And some of the men need medical attention."

The captain sighed. "Alright, we shall head back to Binic. One of the churches in the town has nurses serving in the hospital annex. I've had to avail myself of their services in the past."

Gus patted him on the arm. "Good. Stick to our bargain. A week from today, if I haven't made it to Binic, you sail for England. You go to the Duke of Monsale and tell him what happened."

Monsale would not only ensure that any rumors regarding the sudden disappearance of Augustus Trajan Jones were swiftly dealt with, but he would also handle the delicate matter of informing the Jones family that their son would not be coming home.

Gus took one look at his boat, then clambered over the side. The echoes of more explosions rung in his ears as he headed up the hill.

Evangeline, where are you?

ॄ

Gus was still wiping the dust and sweat from his face when he finally made it up the short rise and into the forecourt of Château-de-La-Roche. Or at least what remained of it.

The roof was mostly gone, and the west wing in which he assumed the gunpowder had been stored was a shattered ruin. Only the rock-solid walls held out.

The fire had now moved to the other side of the château. Gus could only hope that Armand had not stored more powder in that part of the house.

At the bottom of the steps leading up to the front door, he found Armand. He was badly burned. What skin remained on his hands was blackened.

"My friend, you have returned. But too late. There is nothing you can do for me," he said.

"No. Please. You can't die," pleaded Gus.

A sickening crack and almighty crash echoed from inside the château as another part of the roof caved in. No one would be going back in the front door.

Gus bent and slipping his hands under Armand's back, lifted him to a seated position. The Frenchman cried out in pain.

"There is nowhere in the main building which is safe for us. Let me take you into Saint-Brieuc and find a physician," said Gus.

Armand grabbed hold of Gus's greatcoat. "Evangeline.

Where is my niece? They dragged her out of the house and toward the stables. You have to save her. Marec will force Evangeline to become his whore, and if she resists, he will kill her."

The Lamballe gang has Evangeline.

The choice before him was heartbreaking. Leave Armand to die alone or find a horse and go after Vincent and his men. "I will find Evangeline. And I will get revenge for you. I swear that this outrage will not go unpunished."

Armand touched his badly scarred fingers to the back of Gus's hand. "I blew up the château. I would rather destroy it than hand it to a man like Vincent Marec."

No sooner had he said the words, than his body stilled, and his eyes rolled back in his head. A sob escaped Gus's lips. He bowed his head and wept.

Armand La Roche was dead.

Chapter Thirteen

❧

The fire continued to rage on through the rest of the château. Gus ignored it. There was no point in attempting to fight the flames. It was all too late.

Still cradling Armand's body in his arms, he considered his options. The Lamballe gang had disappeared and taken Evangeline. He had no idea where they had gone, but he suspected they were somewhere on the road headed to their camp.

But where?

"Bloody hell," he muttered.

His knowledge of the local area was limited at best. Sir Stephen Moore had always been the one who travelled to the surrounding towns and villages, tasked with collecting the contraband brandy.

"Monsieur Jones?"

Raising his head, Gus was greeted with the sight of one of the estate stable workers. The man held the reins of a brown gelding in his hands. The horse was saddled, with a blanket and bags in place.

Gus recognized the beast. He had ridden the horse a number of times during his earlier trips to the château.

Gently moving Armand off his lap, he lay his friend on the ground, then got to his feet. "Find some of the other servants and have Monsieur La Roche taken to Saint-Brieuc. The head priest at Cathédrale Saint-Étienne will know what to do."

He nodded toward the horse. "Is that for me?"

"Yes. I thought you might want to go after Evangeline. I mean Mademoiselle La Roche. She has the faster horse, so I don't know how long it will take for you to eventually catch up with her."

Gus frowned. *Catch up?*

"What do you mean by that? Doesn't Vincent Marec have her?"

The young man shook his head. "No. She was the one chasing after him. After the château exploded, she took Gobain and galloped off down the road. I noticed she had her rifle in its scabbard as she rode past me. She was going very fast."

Gus felt sick. Evangeline being a captive in the hands of the Lamballe gang was bad enough, but her going after them was possibly even worse.

A grief-stricken young woman more than capable of handling a rifle was a dangerous thing. If she caught up with Vincent and his men, she could well commit murder.

And in retribution the rest of the gang would kill her.

He took the reins from the stable hand. "Do you have any idea where the Lamballe gang are based? I don't know the roads around here."

The lad shrugged. He pointed at the long drive which led toward the main road into Saint-Brieuc. "Go that way. Then at some point on the other side of town, head east. That's all I know."

Gus sighed. Locating Evangeline on the labyrinth of roads which crisscrossed the local countryside was going to be a near impossible task. But he had to try.

He had little money. A single pistol in his coat pocket. And the afternoon sun was sinking low in the sky. Captain Grey and the *Night Wind* would have already sailed out of the river.

Bloody hell. This is a disaster.

A glance back at Armand, who was now being carried to a nearby cart, pushed all doubt aside. He had made a promise to his dying friend. A promise that, no matter how impossible, he had to keep.

"If Evangeline happens to come back, please tell her that I have gone looking for her. I will make for Lamballe and see what clues I can find as to the whereabouts of Vincent Marec and his men."

He slipped his boot into the stirrup and swung his leg up. As he settled into the saddle, Gus did a quick inventory of his coat pockets. A whisky flask, his pistol, and some other bits and pieces. It would have to do.

With a gentle dig in the horse's flanks, he was on his way out of Château-de-La-Roche. A prayer was on his lips as he rode.

Please don't let her find them. She won't show them mercy.

§

You will pay with blood and remorse-filled tears; this I vow.

Fury and rage coursed through Evangeline's veins. It almost blinded her. She could barely see the road ahead for the red veil before her eyes.

"I will kill them all. But Vincent I will save to the end."

She would make him watch as she put a bullet in every one of his men then turned the rifle on him.

Digging her heels in hard, she urged her mount on. One mile, no sign of them. Two miles, nothing. Then Gobain began to flag. He was a magnificent animal, but even he couldn't keep up this punishing pace.

Finally, she pulled back on the reins and slowed him to a

walk. Gobain was breathing heavily. She reached out and patted his neck. It was damp with sweat. It would be cruel to force the horse to continue at a full gallop.

They had followed the road from the château into Saint-Brieuc and were almost on the other side of the town. She hadn't made any progress in finding Vincent and his men. Her mad pursuit had come to naught.

Outside a tavern, Evangeline drew up her horse, letting him drink deeply from a nearby water trough. After dismounting, she stood and pondered her predicament.

The blind rage had subsided, and her mind was slowly clearing. Her thoughts for the past hour had centered purely on finding Vincent and wreaking her revenge on him. With no idea as to where he was, doubt now crept in. Hopelessness quickly followed.

Should she go on or give up and return to the château? Armand was surely dead. It was a miracle Vincent had managed to haul himself out of the ruins of the main house. The fire no doubt would have kept burning, the dry, aged wooden beams and floor of the west wing providing perfect fuel for the flames.

There would be little to salvage if she did return home. And who knew what other caches of gunpowder Armand might well have hidden in the house? Only a fool would venture inside.

Gobain continued to hungrily lap up the water. Evangeline's gaze drifted and settled on her rifle. It had been a gift from her parents on her sixteenth birthday. Her name was engraved on the side.

You packed it; you may as well use it.

Going home would achieve nothing. She had a weapon and ammunition. If she played it smart, she could well take out a number of the Lamballe gang before they knew what had hit them.

But could she really do it? Commit murder. Take the life of another human being.

Evangeline was many things—bold and often fearless—but a killer she was not.

I can't go home without having exacted some sort of revenge. They must pay.

There had to be a way to hurt Vincent, to let him know that he had not gotten clean away with destroying her life. And if he was true to form, the gang leader would have ordered his men to head straight back to their camp just outside Sainte-Anne.

"An eye for an eye," she muttered.

If the Lamballe brutes could come to her home and blow it up, she would go to their hideout and pay them back in kind.

Chapter Fourteen

Sainte-Anne was a hamlet a few miles on the Saint-Brieuc side of the town of Lamballe. There was only a small scattering of houses and no real village to speak of, which made it the perfect place for Vincent and his gang to establish their secret base. No one came in or out of the road which led to the old farmhouse without being seen.

Approaching the camp from the main road was out of the question, but having visited the farm on previous occasions, Evangeline knew another way in.

Leaving Gobain tied to a tree a quarter mile from the site of the camp, she proceeded on foot. The dense shrub land offered excellent cover, allowing her to make it most of the way while remaining hidden from view.

Dropping the saddlebags onto the ground, she crouched low behind a thick hazel bush and considered her options.

There was enough gunpowder in the bags to cause some damage, though not as much as she guessed she would need if she intended to destroy the farmhouse.

I don't want to be an annoying ant; I have to be a bee whose sting remains long in their memory.

Her gaze fell on the two-storied, ramshackle building. The

ground floor was a stone construction, but the top had been built entirely of wood. If she could get a flame established in the upper floor, the whole building would burn.

Evangeline stilled as one of Marec's men carried a crate toward the farmhouse. From the clinking of bottles, she guessed them to be full of brandy.

Now there's an idea. Brandy burns.

If she could set some of the brandy alight and throw in some of the gunpowder, it might be enough to set the place ablaze.

Getting a flame to the brandy and being able to make good her escape was now the biggest problem. She had no intention of letting herself get caught. Revenge was on her mind, not a heroic death.

The sun was slowly setting. Soon it would be dark. And if Marec's men kept to their usual evening habits, they would start heavily drinking the minute they had eaten supper.

The rest of the night would then descend into a progression of loud and tone-deaf singing, followed by a brawl or two, at the end of which most of the gathering would wrap themselves up in their winter coats and fall asleep.

Once the noise had died down, and the men were snoring soundly, she would strike.

Evangeline retreated into the bushes, out of sight. She sat with her back against a large boulder, making herself as comfortable as she could. With her rifle cocked and ready, she settled in to wait.

Before the night was over, she would have her revenge.

Chapter Fifteen

❧

"Bloody woman, where are you?" muttered Gus.

Stubborn was one thing—recklessly seeking revenge an entirely different matter. He dreaded to think what he would do if Evangeline managed to get herself caught by Vincent and his gang. Wringing her neck was the top of his current choices.

It was many hours since he had left Château de La Roche, and he was still no closer to finding Evangeline. He wasn't even sure if he was headed in the right direction.

After coming out of Saint-Brieuc, the main road split at a junction. The wooden signposts, which should have given him a clue as to where to go, had all long faded. Twice now he had followed one road, only to change his mind and come back to the same crossroad.

Now he was lost in the middle of somewhere, surrounded by marshland, and with no idea as to what he should do next.

The *clip-clop* of horse's hooves on the road had him turning in the saddle. Gus sighed as a man clad in a long brown coat and matching leather hat came toward him riding a small mare.

He had been hoping to avoid having to speak to any of

the locals. While his French was near perfect, hiding his English accent was not so easy. But if he was going to have any chance of finding Evangeline, he was going to have to ask for directions. "*Bonjour, compagnon de voyage,*" he hailed the man.

A quizzical look appeared on the man's face. He shook his head. "It is late in the day, so you should say bonsoir. If you are going to speak French, at least try to learn it."

"*Pardonnez mon ignorance,*" replied Gus.

The man waved his apology away. "I used to live in Guernsey, so I speak English quite well. Why are you all the way out here?"

That was a question to which Gus had no sensible answer. "I am horribly lost. I was trying to make my way to the town of Lamballe, but don't appear to be making much headway."

His words got a frown in response. "You are miles away from Lamballe. If you keep on this road, you will end up in Morieux, near the lake." He pointed to the southeast. "Lamballe is five miles as the crow flies in that direction. But, my friend, you will not make it by nightfall. And if you have got lost in the daylight, I would hate to think what will become of you in the dark."

Gus rubbed his worried temple. "So, you are saying that I am best to retrace my steps and go back to Saint-Brieuc and ride out in the morning? I don't know if I can do that. You see I am looking for someone."

"Ah. And the search for this someone cannot wait?"

Gus shook his head. There was a good chance he would be too late to do anything when he did finally catch up with Evangeline, but he had to try. Had to know that before he left France, he had done all he could to help her. "My friend, a local lady, suffered a terrible loss today. She rode off while in a state of great distress. It is imperative that I find her as soon as possible," he replied.

An odd look crossed the other gentleman's face. "Would

this friend of yours happen to be involved in trading goods between here and England?"

Gus shifted the reins into his left hand. His right he moved toward the pocket where he kept his loaded pistol. He tracked the eyes of his fellow traveler as they followed his every movement. "Who are you?"

"My first name is Jodoc. The rest of who I am you don't need to know."

Gus's fingers touched the cold of his weapon and curled around the handle. He was ready to strike at the first sign of trouble.

"But I know who you are, Mister Jones. I am a business acquaintance of Armand La Roche. Or I was if the terrible rumors I heard before I left town are true."

There was no point in denying the truth. "Armand is dead. Killed in a scuffle with Vincent Marec and his men."

Jodoc, whoever he was, didn't need to know the details of what had happened at the château. Armand was gone, and that was all that mattered.

Jodoc slowly nodded. "And Evangeline is the lady whom you seek?"

Gus let his silence be his answer. Jodoc let out a long string of foul expletives.

"If Evangeline went after Marec and his men, which knowing her, she would have done, then there is every chance that she is already dead."

The lump in Gus's throat got stuck partway down. He hadn't wanted to consider what might have happened while he was roaming the back roads of Brittany. Or the insanity that Evangeline might well have unleashed.

He couldn't give up until he knew the truth. If she had indeed met her end with a bullet, he had to know. It was his responsibility to bring her home no matter what.

With a flick of his reins, Jodoc urged his horse closer. Gus kept his fingers on the pistol. The smuggling game was full of two-faced men who would kill you if it meant getting a competitive edge.

"Come back to my house. It is close. I will give you food and shelter. In the morning, I will show you the road which leads to Sainte-Anne. That is where Marec and his men have their base. You don't need to go all the way over to Lamballe to find them."

Gus still didn't trust his would-be good Samaritan. Who was to say Jodoc wasn't in league with Marec and the minute he turned his back, he would betray him?

Jodoc smiled. "You still don't trust me. Good. I am glad to see that you are living up to your reputation."

"Pardon?"

Slowly, the other man moved his hand toward his coat pocket. After dipping his fingers inside, he pulled out a creased and grubby calling card. The instant he held it up, Gus began to laugh.

Discretion assured. Results guaranteed.

In the middle of nowhere, in his hour of need, his fellow rogue of the road had once more reached out and saved him.

"Sir Stephen Moore. Why am I not surprised?" he chuckled.

Was there anyone in the whole of England or France that man didn't know?

Jodoc pointed toward a small farmhouse in the distance. "That is my home. Come."

Gus turned his horse in the direction he had originally been headed and followed his new friend.

In the fast-fading light, there was nothing he could do for Evangeline but pray that she would survive the night.

Chapter Sixteen

The drinking, fighting, and general mayhem lasted well into the evening. From her vantage point, Evangeline observed the goings-on with disgust. She had been blind to all this when Vincent first came into her world. He was a former officer, supposedly an educated man of social rank. Armand had even offered for him to dine with them at the château.

It hadn't taken him long, however, to show his true colors. But by then she had already made a terrible mistake.

Tonight, she was going to correct that error. Erase it from her memory with searing heat and flames.

She searched the gathering; Vincent was nowhere to be seen. He hadn't looked that badly injured at the château, just a little dazed. Perhaps he was lying low or more likely, in Lamballe at some whorehouse celebrating his victory.

Enjoy it because by the time I am finished, it will feel like ashes in your mouth.

Climbing to her feet, she picked up the saddlebags. The rifle she left behind. Then she dashed out from behind the bushes, sprinted across the open ground, and into the dark shadows of the farmhouse. With her back pressed against the stone wall, she waited and caught her breath.

The rowdy noise from the camp continued on unabated. No one had seen her.

Breathe and focus.

Her actions during the next few minutes could well mean the difference between success or facing a horrible death. Her heart thumped hard in her chest, adrenaline pumping through her veins at a fierce knot.

Toward the rear of the building was a small door. Taking great care so as not to make a sound, she tiptoed toward it. When the handle turned silently, she mouthed a silent 'thank you' to Vincent for ensuring that his men kept the campsite in military order. The lock and hinges had been well oiled.

Once inside, she quietly closed the door behind her.

The place was much the same as she remembered from her first and last visit. Crates of brandy were stacked high to the low wooden ceiling, ready for shipment to England.

Evangeline smiled at them. If things went according to plan, those bottles would never leave this place. They would burn.

She worked as quickly as possible, but it still took time to pull most of the crates apart and tip the brandy out. When that was done, she gathered as much straw and hay as she could find and piled it into the middle of the room. It reached the roof. The brandy fumes were so intense in the closed space that it made her cough. She was forced to cover her face with the top of her father's coat in order to muffle the sound.

The last piece of work set before her was to leave a trail of gunpowder from the straw to the door and outside.

By the time she had emptied both saddlebags of their gunpowder, Evangeline had forty feet of fuse line between her and the farmhouse. It wasn't much, but hopefully, it would be enough.

In the dark, flint stone in hand, she paused and considered the ramifications of what she was about to do. If the explosion went as well as she hoped, it would raze the building to the ground. If not, then at least a fire which resulted in considerable damage would follow.

Either way, Vincent would lose an entire shipment of brandy. He would also be without a place to store any future stock.

"That will teach you to come to my home and set a flame to my life."

She struck at the flint, her eyes glistening as the spark caught. The gunpowder sizzled and popped. Then the trail of light was on its way.

Snatching up the saddlebags, she bolted for the woods. It was only when she was well clear of the trees, and in sight of Gobain, that the first *boom* finally rang out through the still of the night.

Reaching her horse, she threw the bags over him, then grabbed at her shoulder, searching for the strap of her rifle. Her fingers, however, touched only the wool of her coat. She spun around; mouth wide open in shock.

Another explosive *boom* echoed. The night sky was suddenly filled with the angry glow of flames.

There was nothing she could do, no going back. After climbing frantically into the saddle, she dug her heels in hard. Gobain leapt away as Evangeline held on tightly to the reins.

"I am sorry, my beauty, but this time I am not going to spare you."

They were many miles farther north of Sainte-Anne before she finally loosened her hold and let the horse catch its breath.

Spearing her fingers through her hair, she cursed her stupidity. *"Espèce d'idiot!"*

She had started a war and carelessly left her calling card behind.

Somewhere in the bushes, just outside the farmhouse, lay her rifle. The one with a griffin and the letters *EBLR* etched beautifully in the metal just above the trigger.

Chapter Seventeen

❦

Would he ever be able to repay the debt he owed to Stephen? The man had not only helped to save his life after he had been shot, but now he had made Jodoc magically appear in the middle of the wild marshes of Brittany.

"If I make it back to England and marry, I shall have to name my firstborn son Stephen," he muttered.

Monsale mightn't like being overlooked in such a way, but he would have to wait. With God's grace a second son would follow, and he could be called Andrew.

Gus had spent the night in a warm bed. His belly was full. It was more than he had expected to have last night before his serendipitous encounter with the jovial Jodoc. Now with the sunrise, Gus had his horse saddled and was ready to leave. His bags were stuffed to the brim with gastronomic delights.

Madame Jodoc—she also wouldn't disclose the family name—had baked some bread late last night. Along with a loaf and a slab of cheese, she had packed salted butter and a jar of sardines.

He wouldn't starve anytime soon.

But food, much as he enjoyed it, wasn't the main priority of his day. Finding Evangeline, or at least discovering what had happened to her, was top of his list. Jodoc had kindly sat down at the kitchen table and drawn up a rough map of the area. It was enough to ensure that Gus wouldn't get lost again.

With his mount ready, he headed back toward the house to say his grateful goodbyes.

Jodoc greeted him in the middle of the farmyard. "You may as well come inside and have another cup of coffee. I have a feeling you won't be going anywhere anytime soon."

Gus glanced up at the heavens. There were rain clouds hanging overhead, but this was Brittany. It rained a lot in this part of France. Getting wet wasn't an issue for someone who had sailed the seas as much as he had. "I can take shelter under trees if I need," he replied.

Jodoc shook his head. "It's not that. You were about to set out to find Evangeline La Roche. Well, she just walked in the front door of my house."

The jolt of relief at hearing that Evangeline was still alive rocked Gus back on his heels. He put a hand over his heart. "Thank heavens."

"I'll unsaddle your horse while you go inside," said Jodoc.

Gus laughed to himself. The way things were going, his second-born was going to be named after the Frenchman.

Monsale, you will have to be satisfied with my third son.

Inside the warm kitchen, he found Evangeline seated at the table, a cup of coffee already in hand. She rose as he stepped into the room.

Jodoc's wife patted Gus on the arm as she passed him by on her way out.

He was grateful for the moment of privacy. "I don't know whether to hug you or put you over my knee," he said.

Tears shone in her eyes as she nodded. "Either one, just as long as you hold me afterwards."

They met in the middle of the room; arms wrapped tightly around each other. The pain of his wound was ignored in the joy of simply holding her. Of knowing that she was still a living, breathing woman. "Where have you been?"

Evangeline drew back, head shaking. "I don't remember half of what happened yesterday. I mean after . . ."

"Armand."

She nodded.

Gus placed a comforting kiss on her forehead. "He is at peace now. They took him to the cathedral of Saint-Étienne, where the estate servants promised to hold a vigil for him. He sent me to find you."

"You mean you felt he would want you to do that?" she replied.

"No. Armand was still alive when we got back from Binic. Critically injured from the explosion, but he lasted long enough to tell me that the Lamballe gang had you. I thought you were their prisoner, but the stable boy explained that you had gone after them."

She put her hand over her face and began to sob. "I waited for him to come out of the château. I thought he was already dead. How could I fail him like that? I should have stayed and tried to help."

"There was nothing anyone could have done to save him. Your uncle was barely alive when I found him. He lasted only long enough to tell me that you had gone."

He was about to make mention of what else Armand had said, but Jodoc marched through the door at that moment. The look on his face was one of great displeasure. Evangeline stepped away from Gus.

"What happened to your horse?" Jodoc's question was directed at Evangeline, and she visibly flinched.

"He threw a shoe last night while I was on the road. As soon as I realized he had gone lame, I dismounted and walked."

Jodoc tutted. "That horse has been ridden hard. There is

dry sweat matted in his mane. Why would you do that to such a fine animal?"

Tears slowly snaked down her face, and Gus sensed she was barely holding her emotions under control. Whatever had transpired the previous evening had left her traumatized and frightened.

"How about I come and give Gobain a full rub down? I can then help you to replace the shoe," offered Gus. He could appreciate Jodoc's anger. Under normal circumstances, he too would take someone to task over mistreating an animal, but in this particular case his main concerns lay with Evangeline.

I need to know what happened to her after the explosion at the château.

Jodoc grumbled something under his breath, then headed for the door. "I'll go and check to see what shoes I have in the stables. I take it from both Evangeline's state and that of the horse, we can't risk taking the horse to the local blacksmith."

"Thank you," she replied.

With their host gone, Gus pulled Evangeline back into his arms. He placed a reassuring kiss on her forehead. "It's alright. You are safe. Now come, sit, and tell me what happened yesterday after you left the château. I spent the best part of the afternoon and early evening looking for you."

Chapter Eighteen

Finding Gus at Jodoc's home had come as quite a shock to Evangeline. She hadn't expected to see him again, so had not put any thought into what she might say if she did.

She had pressed Gobain to gallop long past the point where she knew she should have pulled him up, but fear had driven her on. If one of Vincent's men had caught up with her in the dark, there was every chance they would have shot her on sight.

Resuming her seat at the kitchen table, she studiously avoided Gus's gaze as he pulled up a chair and sat next to her. The time would likely come when she would have to tell him of the events at Sainte-Anne; that time was not now. "How did you end up here?" she asked.

Sir Stephen Moore and George Hawkins were usually the ones to venture inland and deal with the local inhabitants, with Gus remaining either at the château or on his yacht. She hadn't known that he even knew Jodoc.

Gus brushed his hand over hers. "I got lost looking for you. It was a complete piece of good fortune that I happened upon Jodoc on the road late yesterday. I thought he might be an associate of Marec's and was ready to shoot him. That's when he pulled out Stephen's calling card."

Jodoc had been working with her and Armand smuggling brandy and other goods across the channel to England for a number of years. He was one of only a handful of men she and her late uncle had ever fully trusted.

"You didn't answer my question," said Gus.

What am I going to tell him? He will think me mad.

"I chased after the Lamballe gang, but then I realized it was only me against all of them. It would be rash and stupid to go seeking revenge."

Liar.

Gus gave an audible sigh of relief. "I am so glad you decided not to go after them. They didn't destroy the château—Armand did."

Evangeline froze. Had she heard right?

"He told me just before he died. Said he would rather blow it up than let Marec and his villains take it."

A wave of nausea washed over her. Evangeline thought she might throw up. She had exacted fiery revenge when it had been Armand who had destroyed their home.

No. That cannot be true. If it is then . . . Oh dear.

Denial was her only refuge. The truth far too ugly to confront. "That doesn't make sense. Vincent was the one who brought the lit torch into the house, not my uncle. Perhaps Armand was so badly injured that his mind was muddled. He was saying things that were clearly wrong," she replied.

Gus put a comforting arm around her shoulder. "He was lucid, worried about you. But let's not argue about the details. Whoever set the flame to the gunpowder doesn't really matter. The west wing of the château is in ruins. The roof completely gone. The servants had led most of the animals away by the time I reached the courtyard. As for the house, it was too dangerous to go inside."

She picked up her cooling cup of coffee and took a long

sip. Her family home was destroyed, Armand dead. And she had unwittingly sought revenge against someone who hadn't started the fire. The first two facts she knew to be true, the last she wasn't so sure.

Then again. If Vincent hadn't brought the flame into the house . . .

Even if Vincent hadn't actually lit the fuse, he had been the cause of it all. The blame still lay squarely at his feet.

"Evangeline?"

While she was grateful that Gus was here, that he hadn't been dragged into the fight with Vincent, his presence now created a number of problems.

If I could just convince him to go home to England, I might be able to simply disappear.

She had a good horse, some money, and all the reasons in the world to get far away from here. Her cousin Louis was her best option. Making it all the way to Paris would take some doing. Two hundred and seventy miles. It would be a long, dangerous journey, even without a gang of desperate smugglers on her trail.

I have to get away. If they find us, they will think Gus was involved and kill him too.

Only a naïve fool would hold out any hope that Vincent's men wouldn't find the rifle. The burned trail of gunpowder would lead straight to it. She may as well have done the same as Sir Stephen and left a formal calling card.

"Did you hear me, Evangeline?"

She jumped at his words. "Sorry, I am just exhausted. A great deal has happened over the past day." She didn't want to talk about Armand. Couldn't begin to accept that he was gone. Her only remaining family was Louis, and she barely knew him.

"I shall ask Madame Jodoc if you can go upstairs and sleep. When you have rested, then we should talk," said Gus.

Evangeline shook her head. Sleep was a luxury she didn't

have. Getting away from here and taking the danger with her was what mattered. "Thank you, but no. Once Jodoc has put a new shoe on Gobain, I need to leave. If I go now, I should be able to make it to Dinan before nightfall."

A warm hand settled under her chin; Gus turned her head to face him.

Let me go. I am more trouble than I am worth. I will get you killed.

"What is at Dinan? Or more importantly, who?"

She flinched at the obvious hint of jealousy in his tone. Clearing her throat, she attempted to turn away. Gus maintained his hold, light but still firm.

"No one is at Dinan, but it's a sizeable town and I will be able to find lodging there. After that, I can make my way across country and meet with the main road to Paris. I am going to my cousin Louis," she replied.

Gus huffed. "No. You can't just disappear like that into the French countryside. A young woman travelling on her own won't last very long. And yes, I know you have a rifle, but you can't shoot every vagabond between here and Paris."

She stared long into his brown eyes, determined to imprint the memory of them forever in her mind. This was not his fight; she was not his responsibility.

Lifting her hand, she touched where his rough but gentle fingers held her chin.

We will always have that kiss on the beach. That one brief moment when I thought we might have hope for a future together. But that time is now gone.

For many years now she had wondered how it would feel to trace the contour of his short, dark beard. To place soft, tender kisses on his cheek. Her gaze drifted to his lips. A kind smile sat on them. Gus Jones was an intriguing man, handsome in her sight.

"I know you worry about me, Gus. And that is honorable of you. But this is my home, my country. I shall have to trust to the good nature of my fellow citizens and hope I make it to Paris."

The smile on his lips died, replaced by a firm, hard line. "Alright. If you are determined to make the trip, we shall go to Paris. The *Night Wind* will sail for England in a few days, but I should be able to make my way home from the capital. With Europe at peace, it won't be too difficult for me to secure a berth on a ship sailing out of one of the northern ports. Perhaps I might even stay in Paris for a time. See you settled."

She was torn. Having Gus travel with her would indeed be a blessing. Under his protection, she stood a good chance to make it all the way to her cousin's home.

But if Vincent comes after me, then what?

The Englishman might well be a rogue involved in all manner of illegal endeavors, but he was also the sort who would defend her to the death. Enough people she cared about had died. First her parents during a bitterly cold winter, now Armand. She wasn't going to add Gus to that list. "I don't want you to go to all that trouble. Paris will take you far from home. I shall be careful. I will . . ."

He let go of her face and shot to his feet. "Enough! Either I come with you to Paris, or I tie you to your horse and take you to my boat. It's your choice, Evangeline. I made a vow to Armand to keep you safe. You cannot deny the wishes of a dying man."

The determined expression on Gus's face told her she wasn't going to sway him from his demands. "Paris it is then, but we go today. As soon as Jodoc and you are able to get Gobain ready, we should leave."

She was tired and wrung out. The prospect of a long sleep in one of the beds upstairs whispered sweetly in her ear, testing her resolve. It would be so easy to give in and find rest.

By remaining here, she was putting Jodoc and his family at grave risk. They were good people; they didn't deserve to get dragged into the mess she had created. Vincent's men would be on the hunt for her today. In the daylight they would be sure to make ground.

If she was going to have to stand and fight them, it most certainly shouldn't be here. Downing the last of her coffee, Evangeline got to her feet. She stared Gus down. Two could play at the game of stubborn wills. Years of negotiating with smugglers and brigands over contraband had taught her well. "We leave for Paris, and you are not in charge. This is my country; I make the rules."

He followed her out to the stables, his soft laughter still ringing in her ears.

Chapter Nineteen

※

Jodoc made his protests loud and clear. Evangeline was in no condition to be undertaking the long journey to Paris. He even offered for her to come and live at his house. It was no surprise when his generosity was politely refused. She could be stubborn.

Having an iron will, can be a good thing, but in some situations, you have to yield. Bend not break.

Gus wisely stayed out of the argument. He was saving himself for more strategic battles farther down the road. Two hundred and seventy miles with Evangeline wasn't going to be easy.

She was stubborn, yes, but no more than he was. Of greater concern was her lack of tears over Armand. Gus suspected she was still in some form of shock. He had to be there for Evangeline when the dam finally broke. If their relationship was already fractured by dissent, it would make his job all that more difficult.

He was still trying to come to terms with the nature of their relationship. And while Armand had said he wished for Gus and Evangeline to marry, had that really been what he wanted? Getting her to safety may well have been his true motivation. But Gus understood the societal expectations of both France and England. As a gentleman, he would be compelled to offer Evangeline the protection of marriage.

An English smuggler might not have been Armand's first choice of husband for his niece, but he had little choice.

Mid-morning, they set out from the house. Gus huffed as Evangeline pointed her horse's head toward the north. And while he didn't know the country that well, Jodoc's map had given him somewhat of an idea as to where the major towns were and also the general direction in which one had to travel in order to find Paris.

He dug his heels into his mount and caught up with her. "Why are we going this way and not back toward the road leading from Saint-Brieuc? It seems a much more direct route."

She gave him a haughty glare. "As I told you, Dinan is our destination. After there we will travel across country and meet with the main road which leads to Paris. I am not going anywhere near Lamballe. After the events of yesterday, can you just imagine the reception we would receive?"

Gus gave a brief nod, but he still wasn't convinced. If he was Vincent Marec and a well-respected local gentleman had died in his presence, he would be keeping a very low profile. Biding his time until he could safely move to seize Château-de-La-Roche.

But Evangeline would know this, so her reasons for making them travel the narrow back roads to Dinan didn't quite make sense.

She is hiding something.

Secrets were one thing. He and the rest of the rogues of the road traded in them. It was the unknown and unexpected that had a nasty habit of sneaking up on a chap.

And putting a shot in him.

He rubbed at the sore spot on his upper chest. Just the thought of that day in the woods below the château had his wound giving him trouble. He hadn't seen Marec's man until it was too late. "I think Vincent will have other problems to worry about right at this minute. But if you are determined to go this way, we will. Can we at least discuss the planned route once we get into Dinan tonight?" he replied.

Following behind her on his horse, Gus got a clear view of Evangeline throwing her head back in obvious frustration. "Yes, alright. We can talk tonight. Once we find somewhere to stay. I, for one, would love a bed and a long soak in a bath."

Gus let the argument drop. The thought of their travel and accommodation arrangements suddenly presented a larger, more pressing problem. One he hadn't thought of until now. How were they going to present themselves when they reached any of the towns en route to Paris? An unwed couple sharing a room would not pass muster.

We could pretend to be man and wife.

The thought pulled Gus up sharp. They were currently headed to Paris, but nothing was certain. And who knew what lay ahead for Evangeline at the end of that long road if they even made it?

He had a horrible suspicion that Louis La Roche wouldn't be welcoming his penniless cousin with open arms. Someone had to be there for her when she realized that the only thing waiting for them in the French capital was more bitter disappointment.

Gus wanted to be the one she could turn to for comfort.

If Louis cannot help, she will be left with few options. Whatever money he gives her will eventually run out. What skills does a noblewoman smuggler have to offer?

He would be damned if Evangeline was going to end up working as a servant, or worse still, forced to marry some stranger in order to put a roof over her head.

The future they were both headed toward was unknown.

With luck, the next few days would bring some answers. He needed a plan in place for when they eventually reached Paris. One which Evangeline could accept.

What if you could be ready, and willing to offer her another life?

Suddenly, the thought of playing at being Evangeline's husband no longer felt such an odd idea.

Chapter Twenty

✿

She was going to have to tell Gus the truth at some point. Confess her sins. Hopefully, they would be hundreds of miles away before she finally had to share the news of her having blown up Vincent's farmhouse. No matter which way she looked at it, there was never going to be an easy way to say it.

And once Gus had absorbed that shock, she would be compelled to disclose the rest of her secret. The full extent of her stupidity.

Did I forget to mention I left my rifle behind? You know, the one with my name engraved on it.

It was a good thing that they were riding single file. While she grappled with the problem of exactly what to say to Gus, at least she didn't have to look at him.

The ride to Dinan wasn't a particularly long one, but the road was narrow. It was also a thoroughfare for wandering ditch goats and Ouessant sheep, who were not inclined to yield the right of way. More than once, Evangeline and Gus had to dismount from their horses and gingerly walk past a flock of unsociable and grumpy animals.

By the time they reached the hilly outskirts of the

medieval walled town, she was exhausted. Two days without sleep were now finally catching up with her.

She barely lifted her head as Gus rode up alongside her.

"I was thinking," he said, in a tone far too lively for her liking.

"Yes."

"We should get married."

Evangeline pulled hard on the reins, bringing Gobain to a sudden halt. She blinked hard. Perhaps she had fallen asleep in the saddle and was dreaming. "What did you just say?"

He laughed. "I mean, we can't exactly just arrive at any respectable inn and ask to share a room. We need to pose as a married couple. If we don't, we may be refused."

Her shock over his proposal turned to a surprising sense of disappointment at hearing it was only a ruse. What would she have said if he had been serious?

Yes. Perhaps.

A yawn set her mouth stretching wide. She put a hand over her face. "I really need sleep. I am bone weary."

"What do you think?" he continued.

"Yes, we will need to create a façade. But I should do the talking as much as possible. Your French is near perfect, but your accent gives you away. The war might well be over, but outside of the major cities, the English are still not trusted."

It was on the tip of Evangeline's tongue to make mention that anyone who might come looking for her may also inquire as to whether a long-haired Englishman wearing a tricorne hat was in her company. Fortunately, she kept that to herself.

Gus would in all likelihood ask as to why that would be a concern.

And then I might have to tell him the truth.

It would take a solid night's sleep before she would be in any sort of frame of mind to broach that particular subject.

To her relief, Gus simply nodded. "That makes sense. I

don't want to cause any trouble. We just want a hot meal and a comfortable bed."

※

Hotel Vent de Mer was located in the older part of the city, next door to what had once been a Jacobite convent. Evangeline and Armand had stayed at the hotel on a number of occasions. It was a comforting, familiar place. It was also a mistake.

The owners recognized her immediately. She had to make hurried and rather flustered introductions to her *new* husband, Jean Augustin, who was fortunately a man of few words.

Once inside their room, he locked the door behind them. "Jean Augustin? Is that my new name? I thought Augustus Jones wasn't that bad," he teased.

"I'm sorry. I should have chosen a hotel somewhere else in the city. One where no one knows me," she replied.

Merde. Now he will want to know why.

He stepped closer, coming to stand right in front of her. The room wasn't small, but he took up a great deal of space. If his intent was to intimidate her, he was succeeding.

"Why do we need to keep our presence here a secret? Please, Evangeline, whatever it is, you have to tell me."

Her gaze dropped to the floor. The green, knotted wool rug on which they both stood, a sudden source of fascination. "Do you truly believe Armand blew up the château?" she asked.

Gus inched closer. When she breathed in, she caught the hint of his cologne. She had had it made especially for him at a local perfumer in Saint-Brieuc as a Christmas gift the previous year. The woody, aquatic fragrance suited him. Bergamot, citrus, and cedar blended with notes of seaweed and cypress. She closed her eyes and took in a deep breath.

If they were really husband and wife, this moment could be very different. She would be eager for him to hold her after a long day on the road. And her concerns wouldn't be about foolish acts of revenge. Rather, they would be about the two of them sharing a moment of marital intimacy. Of letting her cares and worries melt away while her husband stripped her naked then lay her on the bed. And when he came to her, all she would be thinking of was that sweet sexual climax they would both soon achieve.

If only that was her reality.

"Evangeline, look at me."

With great reluctance, she tore herself away from her private imaginings of him and met his gaze.

"Did you know that Armand was moving gunpowder in secret from Binic? The bottles he sent me to collect didn't contain brandy. They were full of explosives. Armand was building a stockpile of ready-made bombs. He must have stored them somewhere in the west wing of the château."

Evangeline nodded. She had seen the crates, and Armand had told her the truth. It still hurt to think he could do such a thing. Destroy their home. She would forever wonder if he had meant to die in the explosion. To sacrifice himself in order to keep his honor.

Gus tapped his fingers on the front of her coat. "When did you discover about the gunpowder?"

This was too much. Evangeline quickly stepped away, crossing to the window which overlooked the central courtyard and rear stables. A young boy was leading Gobain into one of the stalls, a bucket of oats in his hand. The horse would get a good rub down and a proper night's sleep.

If things didn't go well with Gus, she might not be so lucky.

Warm, strong hands settled on her shoulders, and Gus spun her to face him. There was a kindness in his eyes, a gentle pleading for her to trust him.

"I knew he meant to go to war against the Lamballe gang. I told you as much in my letter. But he was acting very odd yesterday. He couldn't wait to get you back on board your boat and away.

He knew Marec was coming, but he was shocked to discover the rest of the men had also arrived. That was not in his plans. When I found him in the dining room, Armand told me what was in the crates. Then he said I had to pack and leave. Right to the end he was trying to save me. The last time I saw Armand, he was with Vincent. Vincent was the one who had the lit torch, not my uncle."

The open door of the dining room had only been a matter of a few feet away from where the others had been standing. It didn't take much imagination to guess what might have happened. Armand had seen the opportunity to get even with Vincent and had somehow managed to get a hold of the flaming torch.

Evangeline screwed her eyes closed. There was no doubt left in her mind. Armand had destroyed their home rather than hand it over to Vincent. In doing so, he had unwittingly set off a chain of events that was now unstoppable.

"I am so sorry, Evangeline. I cannot begin to imagine how painful this is for you."

She sucked in a deep breath and met his gaze. The moment of truth had finally arrived. "That's not all of it. I lied to you this morning; I did follow Vincent and his men back to their camp at Sainte-Anne. I waited until dark, then I broke in and ruined all his brandy. And I blew up his farmhouse."

Gus's eyes grew wide. He stared at her for a moment, shock written all over his face. "All the saints in heaven, tell me you didn't. Oh, Evangeline," he whispered.

The damage was done. She may as well tell him the last of it. "I rode away as fast as I could. That was why Gobain threw a shoe. He was covered in sweat because I pushed him harder than I have ever done before. All in order to escape."

She put a hand over her eyes, unable to continuing looking at him. The expression of shock on his face was more than she could bear. Shame and hopelessness threatened to overwhelm her. To tear her down completely.

"I am on the run from Vincent and his men. Why? Because I lived up to my foolish and reckless reputation. Not only did I spoil his cargo and burn down his farmhouse, but just to make sure everyone knew how stupid I am, I left my personally engraved rifle behind."

They were on the run for their lives, and it was all her fault.

Chapter Twenty-One

❧

Gus Jones had never been so lost for words. He stood dumbstruck as Evangeline covered her face with both hands and wept. It was several minutes before he finally reached out and pulled her into his embrace.

Holding her, doing his best to offer comfort, he was filled with an almost overwhelming sense of helplessness. In all his years of dangerous endeavors he had never felt so impotent.

In leaving her weapon behind in the woods, Evangeline had all but signed her death warrant. If Vincent Marec and his men found her, they wouldn't show any mercy. They would make her suffer right to the end.

What to do? What the devil are we going to do?

He continued to rub her back long after she too had fallen silent. The only sound to be heard in the room was the low rumble of chatter from the main dining room downstairs. Fellow travelers and local folk enjoying a pleasant drink in the early evening.

Unlike Evangeline and himself, these people had tomorrow to look forward to—they had hope.

"I'm sorry, Gus. I never wanted to put you in this position.

I should have told you before we set out from Jodoc's house. I just didn't know how to," she said.

He shook his head. Now was not the time for regret or recriminations. In his long and sullied career, he had found them to be a waste of time. What was done was done.

She had dug a large hole and thrown them both into it. Now they had to find a way out.

"They will kill us if they find us, won't they?" she said.

It was RR Coaching Company official policy not to lie to one another. If their lives were in danger, he and his fellow rogues of the road had every right to know. And while Evangeline was not a member of the company, she had through contractual bonds established enough rights for the rules to apply in this case.

"Yes, I expect if the Lamballe gang catches up with us, they won't hesitate to shoot," he replied.

Evangeline drew out of his embrace. "Gus, promise me something. If they do find us and things look bad, will you kill me? I would rather die than fall into the hands of Vincent Marec."

I don't know if I have it within me to do that. What you are asking is impossible.

Their desperate situation now revealed the plan to travel to Paris as being beyond dangerous. The capital was still some two odd hundred miles away. And even if by some miracle they did make it, there were no guarantees that they would be safe. From what Gus knew of Louis La Roche, the man was a lawyer, not a soldier.

We have no right to bring war and death to his doorstep.

He had already unknowingly put good people like Jodoc and his wife in peril. Gus was not about to make that mistake a second time. His mind was made up. "We can't go to Paris," he said.

When she lifted her head and their eyes met, Gus's heart

plummeted. He hadn't seen that look of sheer hopelessness since the war. She had already resigned herself to her fate.

No. While there is life there is hope.

"Where can we go? If I return home, they will be waiting," she said.

I need a moment to think.

Evangeline had been honest with him in confessing her attack on the gang. It was only fair that he imparted a piece of his own truth. Of what he had promised Armand.

"I might have an idea. And once I get it straight in my head, we can discuss it. While I figure out the details, I might go downstairs and check on the horses. Now that I know the extent of the threat we are living under, I should make certain that our transport is being well cared for."

Evangeline's face suddenly lit up. She hurried over to her satchel and pulled out a small leather pouch. She offered it to him. "Armand gave me money. A good tip to the stable hand might be in order."

Gus took the coin purse, weighing it in his palm. It was heavy. He untied the strap around the neck of the bag and peeked inside. Gold coins glittered enticingly at him.

If he had been holding any lingering doubts as to whether Armand had planned to destroy Château-de-La-Roche, the coins swiftly removed them. He did a quick count of them, then smiled. "There is at least fifteen hundred francs in here. Enough to get you set up in a new life somewhere far from home."

The gold coins were worth forty francs a piece, more than a month's wages for most French workers. If she remained in France, Evangeline wouldn't starve.

If she remained in France.

He dipped his hand into his coat pocket and withdrew his own meager supply of coins. A few half-francs, two or three full francs, and the rest quarter francs. Not a lot of money, but the right denominations for greasing a palm here or there.

Closing the purse once more, he handed it back to her. "You need to keep that safe. Don't go offering gold coins to anyone. That sort of money will attract the wrong kind of people. I'm going down to the stables; I won't be long."

Gus reached for the door, then stopped. He turned to face Evangeline. Her shoulders were slumped, her whole body a picture of defeat. Under other circumstances, he may well have gone to her, offered more consolation, but he had moved past that point. Their lives were at risk, and he couldn't afford to be weak when it came to her. "Evangeline, what is done is done. We all make mistakes. And believe me when I say that I have made some terrible errors of judgment in my life. Things that have cost lives. I will do all that I can to protect you. But from this moment forward, you must do everything that I ask of you. The time for negotiation is at an end."

She nodded her agreement. "I trust you, Gus. If anyone can get us out of this mess, it is you."

The weight of expectation settled heavily on his shoulders. It was going to take every ounce of his skills and an added dose of luck for them to survive.

How do we make it back to the coast and avoid being caught?

Failure was not an option. Gus was determined that Vincent Marec was not going to get his hands on Evangeline La Roche.

Chapter Twenty-Two

❦

Evangeline wanted a long, hot bath. To soak and indulge herself in peaceful bliss. But in keeping with Gus's instructions for them to maintain a low profile, she settled on a clean cloth and bowl of soapy water. It wasn't what she wished for, but it would have to suffice.

She stripped off her coat and gown, standing naked while she scrubbed at her skin. The traces of sweat, brandy, and gunpowder were slowly washed away. For the first time in days, she almost felt human again.

Now for sleep.

Exhaustion gnawed at her frayed nerves. At least there was the relief of finally having confessed everything to Gus. He hadn't lost his temper, for which she was grateful. Most people would have gone from shock to outrage within an instant, but not him. He had remained calm and in control.

Of course, he did. He has faced untold dangers before.

It took a special kind of man to hold his courage steady when coming face to face with the customs authorities on either side of the English Channel. An ice-cool demeanor which allowed for lies to roll easily off the tongue. And the ability to convince others that he was just a humble sailor who enjoyed life on the sea.

From her satchel she took out a clean gown and laid it on the bed. Then, seated before the tall, thin mirror which hung on the wall, she began the task of undoing the damage which the wind, rain, and hours of riding had inflicted on her hair.

I look like a drowned rat that has been pulled backwards through a water pipe. Thank heavens I packed a brush.

Her long, brown locks were a tangle of knots and frizz. She would give a handful of those gold coins for a maid to assist with repairing the mess.

Slowly but surely, she worked to settle the chaos. By the time Gus reappeared, she had combed her hair and was setting it into loose braids.

He gifted her with a warm smile then turned and locked the door. "I have spoken to the stable boy and given him a quarter franc, with the promise of another before we leave in the morning. He was filling a second pail of oats for our horses when I left."

Evangeline offered her own grin in response. It was such a relief to have Gus with her. She wasn't alone anymore.

After Gobain had thrown a shoe last night, Evangeline had walked for miles along the dark road which led from Sainte-Anne to Jodoc's house. She had wept for some of that time, fearful of what would happen if Marec's men found her and cursing herself for allowing her impetuous nature to overrule good sense.

Every rustle of wind and leaf disturbed had had her peering into the night. Her heart continually racing with the fear that at any moment the thunder of horse's hooves would announce her imminent death.

She set the hairbrush down. The braids would have to do. Fatigue had finally caught up with her.

"Your hair looks nice," he said.

Evangeline rose from the chair, smoothing down her

skirts. The plain gray, woolen gown wouldn't get her an invitation to any fine homes in Paris. It was functional, and that was what counted.

She was no longer the mistress of Château-de-La-Roche; she was simply Evangeline. And if, God willing, she survived the coming days, she would have to come to terms with her new life.

Gus softly chuckled. "No that's not right. Evangeline, you look lovely. A vision of Breton beauty."

She stared at him. Where had that come from? His earlier compliment had given her a private thrill. This second one had her wondering if someone had snatched the real Gus from outside in the stables and replaced him with an exact twin.

If that was the case, she could only hope this version of Gus was as good a fighter as the original.

"When did you start practicing such wonderful encomiums?" she replied.

His soft chuckle went straight to her heart.

If you had any idea what hearing you say those words meant to me, you might blush.

"They are easy when it comes to you, Evangeline. They always have been. It's just that now I feel the time is right to give them voice." There was something in his tone that had her narrowing her eyes at Gus. The hard, warrior was gone—in his place, a gentle lover.

He crossed the floor, and after taking hold of her hand, led her over to the bed and sat her down. She stilled as Gus took a seat beside her.

His fingers now entwined with hers, and he too stilled. "You were brave enough to be honest with me earlier. And now it is time that I do the same with you."

She stared at their joined hands while a hundred thoughts raced through her mind. Was he in league with Vincent? Had he sold her out?

Don't be ridiculous. You are just overtired. This is Gus, and you can trust him.

"I want you to come back to England with me. As my wife." His grip tightened.

England. Marriage. What?

"Don't pull your hand away. Just listen," he said.

He was a strong man. There was little to no chance of her escaping. Her only choice was to remain on the bed.

What he was proposing was, of course, out of the question, but since Gus had promised to do his all to save her life, she at least owed him a fair hearing.

He cleared his throat. Her gaze went to his face, but he wouldn't meet her eyes.

He is nervous.

"You may have noticed that Armand was none too pleased to see me when I arrived at the château. At first, I thought it might be him thinking that my injury would prove a hindrance in any battle. I even toyed with the notion that he wanted to fight Vincent on his own. But then we talked—about you."

"About me?" She didn't like the sound of that at all. Armand had been reserved with her. His taciturn behavior venturing on bloody mindedness. Yet, he had spoken to Gus.

"My arrival here in France threw his plans into disarray. He had intended to send you to England. To me."

Tears pricked at her eyes. Gus didn't actually want her; he was doing a favor for her uncle. He was offering her marriage because he felt obliged.

This was the worst possible outcome for her affections—being bound to a man who didn't care for her, who only saw their union as something sensible.

She had been hungry until this moment, eager to fill her belly with a hot, comforting supper. Her appetite evaporated. The large, heavy swell of disappointment which now sat in her stomach left no room for sustenance.

This was, however, was not a done deal. She couldn't be forced into marriage. Gus had no legal hold over her.

I can't do this to him. Spend a lifetime with a man I love, when he only sees me as . . .

No. She couldn't. Wouldn't. No.

"I release you from all and any undertakings that you may have made to my uncle. Armand was not right in his mind. It wouldn't take much to have a physician attest to that fact, especially since he confessed to destroying his own home," she replied.

Gus finally met her eyes. "Do you find the thought of me being your husband that distasteful? If you do, then I won't press my suit."

He rose from the bed and knelt in front of her. "I have always liked you, Evangeline. And I must confess to having harbored a secret tendre for you these past few years. As I said, I came to France for you. That kiss we shared on the beach was as honest as I have ever been with someone."

She wiped her sudden tears away with the sleeve of her gown. This was all so unexpected. And too much. Was Gus simply being kind? If so, then her answer must surely be no.

But what if he does really want me? If his feelings are more than just a warm regard?

Their private moment in the chapel and the cove had been before Armand's return. Gus couldn't have known about her uncle's plans when he'd kissed her.

I cannot think. I am tired and bone weary with grief.

"Gus, I can't give you an answer tonight. I am not in any condition to make such a life-changing decision. When we reach our final destination, wherever that is, then we can talk further and settle the question of your marriage proposal."

Who knew? Maybe a few days travelling with her would cure Gus of any foolish notions of making her his wife. Then again, it may not.

"Alright. I shall go downstairs and see what supper we can find. A good night's sleep will help us both."

After Gus was gone, Evangeline remained seated on the bed. Her eyelids grew heavy, and she lay on her back, intending to grab a few minutes sleep before he returned.

When he did return, Evangeline was roused from a deep slumber to find him bearing two bowls of stew and a small loaf of bread. She rolled over onto her side. "Hmm. It smells delicious. Is that cotriade?"

He bent and placed a soft, tender kiss on her cheek. "Yes, Mademoiselle Sleepyhead, it is. Come and eat."

His gentle words and easy affection stirred the longing within Evangeline. She had been doing her best to keep it quiet, let it also sleep soundly. Rising from the bed, she met his grin with her own shy smile.

He had removed his tricorne hat and the long, dark wig. It was rare to see his real hair. It was similar in color to the false hairpiece, but short and neat. Having seen him in his disguise for so long, she found the authentic Gus Jones a revelation.

Her fingers itched with the need to touch his hair, to brush the soft curls which now slowly unfurled after their release. And if she did that, would he stop her? Or would he allow her to explore, perhaps even place a kiss on that spot just below . . . oh.

A rush of heat raced down her spine. She was seeing Gus in a new light. Being sweet on him all this time had been her own private passion. To think that he might want to share a life with her, well, that was something entirely unexpected.

But welcome?

What if they could forge a future together, a real marriage? It would likely mean her having to leave France for good. To follow in the footsteps of the other French émigrés who had fled to England during the revolution.

She had much to think about over the next few days. This decision could not be made in haste.

Accepting the spoon Gus handed her, Evangeline took a seat opposite to him at the small table by the window.

The cotriade tasted as good as it smelled. The fish was tender, the potatoes soft and soaked in garlic. The stew had been poured over a toasted baguette, which she broke up with her spoon.

They ate in companionable silence for a time, exchanging shy smiles as they slurped their supper.

Gus picked up his bowl and drained the last of the stew before setting his bowl on the table. "That was delicious. Nothing beats a Breton cotriade. And believe me when I say I have indulged in my fair share of soups and stews over the years."

She leaned forward, studying him. Gus had travelled far and wide, she knew that much about him. Seeing him without his usual disguise set her mind to wondering what else there was to this man. Aside from family friend and fellow smuggler, she didn't honestly know him.

There was the obvious attraction. It had been there for some time, for as long as she could remember.

I want to know more. I need to know. If he wishes to offer marriage, it can't be to a stranger.

"It occurred to me that I don't know much about you other than snippets of what you and your friends have told me over the years. Whichever destination we choose, we have a long road ahead of us. So, be forewarned, Gus Jones, I plan to put that time to good use," she said.

"Well then it is a fortuitous thing that you already know the best about me. Smuggler. Professional liar. Occasional thief. It's a wonder I haven't already been snatched up by a good woman, I have much to offer."

Stifling a laugh, she dipped her spoon into the stew. "Your family must be so proud."

Thank heavens you don't already belong to another woman.

Chapter Twenty-Three

❧

She hadn't said no. As a man used to dealing with tight situations and narrow escapes, Gus had a warm appreciation for even the slightest hint of hope.

If Evangeline wanted to spend the next few days grilling him about his life, he would be more than happy to indulge her.

The more she knows, the more considered her decision will be.

He pushed away his disappointment at having not received a gleeful yes in response to his proposal. Evangeline's response was understandable. And a small room in an inn wasn't exactly the most romantic of places.

I expect she would have imagined a château full of blooms and a poetic declaration of love.

Then again, young ladies didn't usually go about setting fire to smuggling gang's brandy caches and blowing up farmhouses.

With supper finished and their dishes cleared away, sleep now beckoned. There was a small argument regarding who was to have use of the bed, at the end of which Evangeline stood firm. They would both share the comfortable straw mattress.

"As you said, you are an unashamed rogue, so why start trying to be a gentleman just because you want to get my agreement to marry you? Besides, if we do marry, we will be sharing a bed every night, so a spot of practice won't do us any harm."

Gus averted his gaze, worried that the lustful thought which had just popped into his mind might inconveniently reveal itself on his face.

If we do marry, sleep won't be our first priority. And you will get lots of practice in testing the comfort of a bed.

He made a mental note to quietly test the waters regarding Evangeline's knowledge of marital matters. She had lived on a farm most of her life, so she must have some idea as to what happened with animals. Her education as far as humans went, however, was less certain.

Evangeline climbed into bed, still dressed in her gown, and threw the blanket over herself. Gus made use of a clean bowl of water, washing his face, checking his saddlebags, and generally delaying the moment when he would have to lay beside her.

He wasn't used to sharing a bed with a woman without the both of them being naked. This was strange.

Clad only in his shirt and trousers, he lifted the blanket and settled in next to Evangeline. She rolled over and faced him. "This is a small bed. I must warn you I like to sleep on this side. I hope that won't disturb you."

The thought of watching her while she slept was all too tempting. If he did, there was every chance that his mind would take to wandering again. To those places where he indulged in his secret fantasies of her.

His manhood twitched its approval.

Gus moved to lay on his back. If his wound didn't give him such pain and trouble, he would have turned fully over and faced the window. Staring up at the low whitewashed ceiling was the best he could manage.

Evangeline moved closer, snuggling against him. When she draped an arm over his waist, Gus closed his eyes. The scent of soap and the trace of her light, floral perfume filled his senses.

"Thank you for not being angry with me over what I did to Vincent's camp. Or if you are mad, I am grateful that you didn't yell at me. What I did was reckless. It may yet get us both killed. If it does, I just want you to know how sorry I am."

With her being this close, Gus was struggling to breathe, let alone talk. His burgeoning erection was making its demands loud and clear in his head. If Evangeline's hand moved just an inch or two lower on his stomach, he might have some serious explaining to do.

With a tired sigh, Gus wrapped his fingers around hers and shifted them higher. "It's done. Try and get some sleep. We can talk in the morning."

He gritted his teeth and began to mentally count brandy bottles.

Un. Deux. Trois.

It was going to be a long night.

Chapter Twenty-Four

※

"Let me see if I have this correct. After we leave Dinan this morning, we take the road leading northwest which passes through Plancoët, then turn west, eventually coming out onto the main Saint-Brieuc coastal road on the other side of Lamballe?"

Evangeline nodded. "And for that last piece of the journey we ride at night doing our best to avoid meeting anyone."

The decision had been made. If they wanted to live, Paris was not an option. They would turn round and make a run for the coast.

If they could make it safely as far as the outskirts of Saint-Brieuc, they would bypass the town as best as possible, then strike fast for Binic. Hopefully, the *Night Wind* would still be in port, waiting for them.

And if Evangeline had chosen the path Gus hoped she would, they would both be getting on board the yacht and sailing for England.

"There is one thing we haven't discussed," she added.

Gus had been dreading this, praying that Evangeline wouldn't ask it of him. "Armand. You want to go and visit him at the cathedral in Saint-Brieuc. Is that what you were going to say?"

Evangeline picked at her small breakfast roll, breaking off a piece. She studied it for a moment. "I owe it to him to at least say goodbye."

Armand had taken care of his niece since the untimely deaths of both her parents during a typhus outbreak one terrible winter. He could understand her position.

But he also appreciated the danger that might well put them both in. Vincent Marec would no doubt find out where Armand's body had been taken and have eyes watching the cathedral. They couldn't risk it.

There has to be a way for us to pay homage to him before we leave.

"Then again, he would be most displeased with me if I managed to get us both killed simply because I wanted to see his casket," she said.

Gus held back his words, not wishing to push her in any direction. If he said no, Evangeline might well hold it against him at a later juncture. And if he said yes, and they did get caught by the Lamballe gang, he doubted he would be able to save them.

A lot rested on her decision.

"Much as I want to say a fond farewell to Armand, it would be unwise of us to go to the Cathédrale Saint-Étienne. I have already done one foolish thing this week, let's not add to that tally."

Gus could have wept with relief.

"If we do make it to Binic in one piece and there is time, we could go to one of the local churches and hold a prayer service for him. Armand was obviously fond of the town. I expect he would like that," he replied.

Her head lifted and she met his gaze. "Yes, the Notre-Dame de Bon-Voyage chapel is close to the waterfront, along

Rue des Écoles. We could go there—time and danger permitting."

Matters settled; Gus picked up his saddlebags. Their food supplies had been replenished and his hip flask was once more filled with brandy. With his coat, wig, and hat all back in place, he looked every part the local country gentleman. The perfect disguise.

As soon as Evangeline was finished with her breakfast and ready to leave, they would be headed on the road out of Dinan and into the wilds of Brittany.

"Don't be long. We need to cover as many miles as we can today. We have to plan for contingencies once we get closer to the coast. Who knows what Marec might have waiting for us? And Captain Grey has a set timetable for departure; he won't stay in port any longer than needs be," he said.

He dreaded to think how skittish the men on board the boat would be right now. Château-de-La-Roche had been blown to pieces. And they were being asked to stay in Binic and wait patiently to see if the elusive Mister Jones made an appearance. He hoped the crew of the *Night Wind* had emulated the Boston Tea Party and thrown the crates of gunpowder overboard.

They probably think I am already dead.

Outside in the stables, he went to check on the horses. The coins he had given the stable boy last night should have resulted in the best of both feed and stalls for his and Evangeline's mounts.

He had just stepped into Gobain's stall when the lad he had tipped last night suddenly appeared from around the other side of the horse. Gus's cheery greeting never made it past his lips. The young man held a finger up and slowly shook his head. He motioned for Gus to follow him.

He led Gus to the back of the stall. "There are some men who have just arrived, and they were asking me about any other travelers who were staying at the hotel. One of them mentioned a young woman with chocolate brown hair," whispered the boy.

Ruddy hell.

"Where are they now?" Gus asked.

The boy pointed to the far end of the stables. "They have left their horses and gone to the nearest public house to eat and drink. Once they are finished, I expect they will come back here and ask more questions."

Gus leaned in. "What did you tell them about the woman?"

If the men were as he suspected, part of the Lamballe gang, they would be looking for Evangeline. Her manner of dress and noble bearing made her stand out in any crowd.

"I told them nothing of her. They treated their animals poorly. And they said harsh things about Mademoiselle La Roche. They called her a whore. Said that she was going to get more of what she had already had, but that this time she wouldn't enjoy it. A man who is harsh to simple beasts and women is not to be trusted. I told them the only people who stayed here last night were two gentlemen on their way through to Rennes."

Gus didn't like what he was hearing, both about Evangeline and also the stories the lad had been telling. "Why did you lie to them?"

He shrugged. "The voice of feeling cannot lead us astray; and one can never be guilty for following nature."

When Gus frowned, the boy sighed. "Évariste de Forges de Parny. My tutor makes me study him. I used to think his poems were boring, but I am beginning to understand them."

A stable boy with a tutor?

"My father owns this hotel; he wants me to have an education, so I can look after him when he is old."

"He is a smart man. Now which way did these men go?"

"Out the front, across the street. If you are looking to avoid them, which I suspect you are, then Mademoiselle La Roche will not be able to come down the main stairs. And to make your troubles even worse, the back ones are broken, and the carpenter isn't coming until next Tuesday."

Which meant the only way for Evangeline to safely leave the hotel was for her to climb out the window.

Merde.

The choice now set before him was whether to risk her using the main stairs and being seen or shimming down one of the old clay downpipes. Neither appealed.

"My father is a good man but a little too effusive if you get my meaning. The moment those men set foot inside, he will happily tell them everything. Mademoiselle La Roche has stayed here many times over the years; he is sure to mention her. And of course, you."

Gus fished in his coat pocket and pulled out a one-franc coin. The boy had more than earned it. "Thank you but promise me you won't tell those men any more lies. Just say you had forgotten if they happen to mention Mademoiselle La Roche again."

He and Evangeline now had to make as hasty and discreet a departure as they could.

"Would you lead our two horses into the rear lane and wait for us there? We shouldn't be long. Then we will take our problems with us and leave your family in peace." Gus turned and headed toward the front of the stall. As he stepped into the yard, he bent and picked up a handful of small stones.

"Monsieur, one last thing. The men. The tall one. He was the one who smacked his reins over the face of his horse. His scar-faced companion addressed him as Vincent."

Gus clutched the pebbles tightly in his hand.

He had taken several more steps toward the back of the hotel, ready to toss pebbles at the window of his and Evangeline's room, when a loud whistle echoed through the yard. Whirling round, he caught sight of the boy, pointing frantically toward the walkway which led from the front of the hotel into the stables.

A risky glance confirmed Gus's worse fears. Vincent Marec and one of his crew had just stepped out of the tavern across the road and were headed this way.

"Go! Take the horses. I will get Evangeline!"

He dropped the small stones and picked up a sizeable rock, took aim, and launched it at the window of his and Evangeline's room.

※

Evangeline checked herself in the mirror one last time. It wasn't the best that she had ever looked, but it would have to do. The coffee and food had been excellent and were settling nicely in her stomach.

From the happy way Gus had bustled about their room earlier, it was clear he had managed to get some sleep. She had got a few hours rest in the hour or two before dawn. Before that, she had lain awake for what felt like the longest time simply watching Gus as he slept. The glow from the flames in the fireplace had softly lit the room. His chest had risen and fallen with his breathing, the steady beat a comforting cadence.

She had intended to turn over and try sleeping with her back to him, but sometime in the middle of the night he had slipped an arm around her, and not wishing to disturb his deep slumber, she had remained where she was.

It had been nice, being held by him. Comforting.

"Now we just need to get some miles behind us today without any trouble."

Gathering her things, she picked up her coffee cup and drained the last of it.

Good coffee should never be allowed to go to waste.
CRASH!

The window of their room exploded. Shards of glass shattered everywhere. A series of stones quickly followed through the new hole. Whoever was in the yard was clearly determined to get her attention.

Leaning over the table she peered out. Down below, she caught sight of Gus waving his arms frantically above his head. When their gazes met, he put a finger to his lips. She nodded. He wanted her to be quiet.

If you were going for subtle, why did you just heave a rock through the window?

He pointed at her, then at the ground.

He wants me outside. Alright.

Another stone made its way into the room. Evangeline huffed. "This is ridiculous. If you want to play charades, you are not supposed to be using projectiles."

She shuffled the table to one side and poked her head through the hole in the glass. Gus was now standing right below it.

"*What?*" she mouthed.

"Vincent and one of his men are here. They will probably be talking to the innkeeper and asking about you. I'm afraid that there is nothing else to do but for you to climb down," he called in a hurried whisper.

Evangeline quickly unlatched the window frame and swung it fully open. It was a good ten feet to the courtyard below. Not high enough to kill her, but if she didn't hit the ground cleanly, there was a risk that she could injure herself quite badly. "Oh, sweet heavens, what am I to do?" she muttered.

Gus gestured toward the window ledge and the nearby drainpipe. Evangeline took one look at it and vehemently shook her head. The pipe was old, possibly the original one from when Hotel Vent de Mer had been built.

THE ROGUE AND THE JEWEL

Her choices, however, were limited. If she stayed in the room, she was dead. The climb out the window, while also suicidal, at least gave her a remote chance of survival.

She hitched up her skirts, tying a rough knot in the gathered fabric. It wasn't the best solution, but at least it would stop her gown from catching on the broken glass or her hem getting in the way.

The window was a tight fit. She squeezed feet first through the narrow gap, doing her best not to get impaled or cut by the sharp fragments.

With the toes of her boots the only thing with any real purchase on the ledge, she shuffled along until she reached the drainpipe.

The whole time she undertook this insane endeavor, she was the subject of Gus's fevered whispers. "Hurry. You must hurry."

I am hurrying. Just trying for it not to be to my death.

With her fingers and boots clutched tightly to the clay moldings, she sent a prayer to heaven, then dropped.

He caught her just before she hit the ground. "Oof."

They both tumbled heavily onto the hard stone of the courtyard. Gus let out a low string of vile expletives, some of which Evangeline hadn't ever heard before. And she had been around smugglers and sailors almost all her life.

He struggled to his feet, clutching at his wounded shoulder. His face contorted in agony. Evangeline winced as she stood and tried to put weight on her right ankle.

"Let me look at your shoulder," she said, ignoring her own injury.

"We don't have time. They could be here at any moment," he said.

Evangeline hobbled after him as he hurried toward the rear lane way where the stable boy and their horses were waiting. After struggling onto their mounts, they quickly rode away.

They had escaped, but barely. A minute or two later and they would have been discovered.

And then what would we have done?

The journey back to the coast and the *Night Wind* had just become a flight into danger.

Chapter Twenty-Five

Evangeline's father had taken her on several long journeys over the countryside as a young girl. France had been in turmoil. First with the aftermath of the revolution, and then with the ongoing political strife that had seen them lose their home for several years. It was her memories of the roads they had travelled during those trips which she now drew upon.

It was a painfully slow ride out of Dinan. They dared not draw attention to themselves, so they joined a small group of fellow travelers who were also leaving the walled city. They waited until they had ventured a good five miles from the town, before finally breaking away and striking out on their own.

Turning off the road, they made their way up a narrow track and into a woodland area. Once they were far into the trees and out of sight, Evangeline pulled back on her reins and brought Gobain to a stop.

Gus drew up alongside her on the bay. "Well done. We got away."

"For now."

He threw a leg over his saddle and dropped to the

ground. He held out his hands as he came to the side of Evangeline's horse. "Let me help you down."

She shooed him away. "It's just a sprain. I can get off a horse without assistance. The last thing you should be doing is putting pressure on that shoulder. I know your injury was stirred up when we fell. So, don't go getting all heroic on me, Gus Jones."

"It's fine. Just a little sore. The doctor I saw in London says I will likely never have full use of this arm again, so I may as well get used to the discomfort."

She climbed down from Gobain, giving Gus a dirty look when he reached out and steadied her as she landed.

"Do you want to remove your boot? I could examine your foot," he offered.

"When I last looked it was still improper for a gentleman to peek at the ankle of a lady. So, thank you but no. Besides, I have a feeling that once I take this boot off, I won't be able to get it back on. My ankle has already swollen enough to be pressing against the sides."

A patch of red appeared on Gus's cheeks. It was rather sweet that he was embarrassed over offering to lift her skirts and take a look. She limped over to a nearby tree and plopped onto the grass.

There was a small pond nearby and Gus led the horses over to it and let them drink. Returning to Evangeline, he sat down beside her. After pulling his hip flask from out of the pocket of his greatcoat, he bent and waved it under her nose. "Something for the pain."

The warm brandy slid easily down her throat. While Gus took his own drink, Evangeline lay against the bottom of the tree trunk. She still didn't want to consider how close they had come to being caught at the hotel.

"What are we going to do? I doubt Vincent and Claude are going to leave Dinan without a clear idea as to where we might have gone. The innkeeper will have confirmed my identity, and possibly yours," she said.

Gus put the lid back on the hip flask and tucked it into his pocket. "Vincent isn't a fool. It won't take him too long to work out the real identity of the gentleman you are travelling with."

He wasn't wrong. Vincent and his second in charge, Claude, had fought Gus and Evangeline during the gun battle several months ago. Claude had been the one who had shot Gus. And just about everyone in Saint-Brieuc knew the group of Englishmen who regularly visited Château-de-La-Roche from time to time.

"We may have eluded them on our way out of the city, but it won't be long before he realizes that we are not on the road to Paris," he said.

꼐

The mention of Vincent brought back the words of the stable boy. Of what had been said about Evangeline. He was about to raise the subject, when she suddenly put her hands over her face and let out a low, heart-rending keen.

"He's dead. Armand is dead. I can't believe it has truly happened," she sobbed.

Gus wrapped his arms around Evangeline. Her whole body shook as she wept for her uncle.

He knew exactly what was happening. She had been on the run for two days. Adrenaline had kept her going. Now as they sat in the quiet still of a country lane, things had finally caught up with Evangeline. She had stopped, and her world had come crashing down.

Gus had lived through war. Had known men to continue fighting long after the battle was over, their minds unable to accept the truth of what their eyes beheld. Even the rogues of the road had suffered these dreadful moments. The pain which came when reality and the mind finally fused in the heat of realization was shattering to the soul.

"I'm sorry, Evangeline. I wish I had been there to talk him out of it. To have been standing beside him when Marec arrived."

Against his chest, her head moved back and forth. She pulled away, and he met her reddened eyes. "When I told him, Vincent was approaching, he barely batted an eye. He knew he was coming yesterday. Armand was trying to protect both of us. That's why he sent you to Binic. He wanted you to be far away when the showdown with Marec occurred."

He must have sent word for Marec to come and take the château. It was all prearranged. But why?

No one would ever fully understand why Armand had destroyed the château. Had it been for the sake of his honor? Or to exact revenge? The dead couldn't answer for their actions. Armand had taken his whys and wherefores with him to the grave.

She wiped her tears away, and softly sighed. "What do you honestly think of our chances of making it to Binic alive? Vincent has never been one for doing things by halves. Or at least not when he can help it."

Gus looked away, searching for the right words. There was an old connection still existing between Evangeline and Vincent. It was something he hadn't realized until now. He didn't understand it, nor did he like it. But he had to know the truth.

"You are truly afraid of Vincent Marec. What is it with you and him?"

Jealousy burned in his stomach. He hated himself for feeling this way when she was still so fragile over Armand.

I am a cad of the worst kind.

She sat back, drawing her knees up. "He is a mistake that keeps coming back to haunt me." Lifting her head, she met his gaze. The pain in her eyes said it all, and Gus's heart sank.

"Years ago, before you and I met, Vincent and I were close for a brief time. I broke it off, and he has never forgiven me. He is not a man accustomed to having women tell him 'no', especially after they have . . ." Her voice cut off with a choked sob.

A flash of primal rage sparked in Gus's brain. Every nerve in his body was set to explode.

Gus got to his feet. He was in need of a walk. As he headed toward the trees, he reached into his coat pocket and let his fingers settle on the trigger of his pistol.

Fury simmered just below boiling point. Vincent Marec might well be on the hunt for them, but at that moment, he should consider himself fortunate not to have located his quarry. If Gus ever saw Vincent again, he was going to kill him.

Chapter Twenty-Six

Evangeline wasn't surprised by Gus's reaction. He could read the meaning in her words. She and Vincent had been lovers. And while their affair had been brief, and most definitely not sweet, the fact that she had been with another man was more than likely giving the Englishman reason to rethink his marriage proposal.

She sat waiting for Gus to return. While her injured ankle did hurt, she could have got up and followed him. Common sense told her to stay put.

If his offer is rescinded, then so be it. I won't be judged by anyone.

And if that was the case, and Gus no longer wished to make her his wife, then she should be grateful. A man who could think poorly of a woman for her past mistakes was not a man she would want to be bound to for the rest of her life.

By the time Gus finally made his way back to where she sat, Evangeline had made up her mind. And she had the basis of a plan. She would go with him to Binic, then find a ship to take her farther up the coast toward Le Havre. In time, she would make her own way to Paris and her cousin, Louis. Problem solved; marriage obligations averted.

He approached, wearing a determined expression on his face. In his hand were the hat and wig. Whatever he was about to say, she could tell it was going to be serious and honest. All the pretenses of his smuggler personae had been put aside.

He set his things on the ground then went down on bended knee. Evangeline braced herself for what was to come.

"I have had a think," he said.

"So have I," she replied. Rather than have them both suffer through the awkwardness of Gus withdrawing his offer of marriage, it made sense for her to release him from his obligations. To restate her position of the previous day.

"I thought we agreed that I was in charge of this mission. One of the benefits of being the leader is that I get to speak first. Well, some of the time, at least."

His gentle rebuke had Evangeline staring at her lap. She was still looking down, unwilling to meet his eyes, when he took hold of her hand.

"Thank you, for your honesty. You trusted me enough to share something that I suspect you have not told another living soul. Forgive me if my first reaction was that of anger. It was not aimed at you. In truth, I must confess to being jealous. But that is my problem to deal with, not yours."

"I never loved him. It was a foolish infatuation that died almost as soon as it began. Once he believed I was his, he showed me his true nature. Vincent isn't an evil man, but neither is he good."

Gus brushed his hand over her cheek and smiled. "What Marec is doesn't matter. He is your past. And if you are prepared to accept me, I would gladly be your future."

He still wanted her.

"Are you sure? I mean, I don't want you to feel compelled just because of the situation we find ourselves in. I can take a boat from Binic and find my own way to Paris," she replied.

He leaned in and placed a soft kiss on her lips. "The only boat, ship, or yacht you will be sailing from Binic in is mine. And that will be after you have become my wife."

We will marry in France?

"You and I talked about holding a service at the church in Binic for Armand. Why don't we have two services? A wedding and a prayer vigil. It will be the closest thing to him being there."

Gus had put considered thought into this, both the proposal and the wake for her uncle. If anyone should be feeling humble, it was her.

Evangeline swallowed deeply. Whatever Gus truly felt for her, she trusted that he wouldn't ever lie. Their relationship was evolving at a fast rate; and while she knew the depth of her own feelings for him, it only made sense that Gus would need time to come to terms with his emotions. "And you are sure about this?"

Gus rose over her, placing his hands either side of Evangeline's face. "Yes. Say you will be mine."

"Yes."

His mouth met hers. The warmth and tenderness of his kiss, both surprising and delightful. When his tongue slipped past her lips, she moaned.

She clutched at Gus's coat, holding him to her. They might be in the middle of a field, but she had no intention of releasing him. Not until he had thoroughly kissed her.

I could do this all day.

They were both panting when finally, reluctantly, they broke the embrace.

"If I had known you kissed like that, I would have been waiting for you at the jetty every time the *Night Wind* arrived. And I would have stopped you going into Saint-Brieuc," she said.

You didn't think I knew about you and the crew. About your visits to the local taverns.

He nervously cleared his throat. "Those days are now behind me. I am in possession of a fiancée, and soon she will be my wife. All my kisses and embraces belong to her."

She tapped her finger on the end of his nose. "Good. I shall hold you to that, Gus Jones."

Gus was still grinning at her when he moved to sit back on the ground. But as soon as he thrust his arm out to steady himself, his smile instantly disappeared. He was clearly in pain.

"Can I take a look at it for you?" she asked.

"It's not fully healed from the shot, and that tumble we took at the hotel didn't help. I'm not sure what you can do for it, apart from offer sympathy," he replied.

She narrowed her eyes at him. "As you said not five minutes ago, I am your fiancée. That gives me rights. One of which is to take care of you despite your protests."

Evangeline got to her feet.

"I will get some cold water from the pond. While I am gone, you should remove your coat and jacket."

The smile returned to his face. "Oui, Madame Jones."

Chapter Twenty-Seven

Only a fool would refuse when a beautiful woman offered to touch him. And Gus Jones was no fool. If Evangeline wished to enforce her rights to lay her hands on him, who was he to deny her?

While Evangeline went to the pond to get the water, he did as he was told and removed his outer garments. His injured arm protested as he slipped it out of his jacket sleeve. A small dose of laudanum would be most welcome right now.

She returned carrying a small leather bucket. Gus gave it a second glance. "Weren't you using that to carry water for the horses?"

A derisive snort was her answer to his question. "What happened to the hardened sailor? Don't tell me those weeks in convalescence have made you soft. Perhaps I won't marry you after all. One life-threatening incident and you go all to pieces."

Mischief and mirth danced in her eyes.

"If you come closer, I will show you just how hard I am," he replied.

She stood staring at him for a moment, those plump pink

lips of hers slightly open. He was tempted to ask what she was thinking. He had a pretty good idea. It was written all over her face. When she ran her tongue along her bottom lip, his manhood sprang to attention.

Get a hold of yourself. You still have a long way to go today. And you are far from out of danger.

Much as he craved to share an afternoon of lovemaking with Evangeline, this was not the time nor the place for it. "Please put the cold compress on my shoulder. I promise to behave," he said.

She knelt beside him and for the first time, he sensed a touch of shyness about her. They had progressed their relationship today. Decisions had been made. But they were mere words. The warm touch of a future lover was a potent thing.

He lifted his shirt, wincing as he pulled it over his head.

From out of her satchel, Evangeline produced a small cloth. After dipping it in the bucket, she lightly wrung it out, then moved closer. "This is going to be chilly, but it will give you some relief." Laying the cloth over the angry red scar of his wound, she fell silent.

Gus placed his hand over hers. "Thank you. And yes, it does help. Then again, anything you do is good."

A tear landed on the back of his hand, and he glanced up. She was crying.

"I feel so guilty over you getting shot that day at the château. I had to hold back on firing my weapon in case I hit you. But all it did was get you injured anyway," she said.

He leaned in and brushed a kiss on her cheek. "It wasn't your fault. In the middle of a gun battle, people are going to get hurt. Or worse."

Gus wasn't ready to confess that his getting shot had been as a result of his own stupidity. He had been too concerned with moving the shipment of brandy back to the boat. Not paying enough attention to the signs of trouble. In the end, he had panicked and paid the price.

Thank god Stephen had had the presence of mind to abandon the cargo and get the boat ready to sail. Gus had scant memories of actually getting back on board or them sailing away from the château.

All I do remember is the pain and the screaming.

There was nothing worse than hearing a grown man crying out for his mama only to realize that the words are coming from your own mouth.

Evangeline pulled the cloth away and dipped it into the water once more. "The wound looks like it was stitched well. It didn't get poisoned?"

Gus shook his head. "Captain Grey held me down while he cut the shot out. Then he closed the wound. When we got back to London, Stephen's wife, Bridget, checked and cleaned it."

"You were very brave. When I brought you down to the yacht on my horse, I feared you might die. I spent weeks waiting for word that you had survived."

He sighed. Getting a message to the La Roche's had been a particular problem. The other rogues of the road had all been busy with their own lives and concerns. None had the time to travel to Portsmouth, let alone France. Monsale's ongoing issues with the French authorities precluded him from getting anywhere near the country. "I'm sorry, I couldn't send a letter. The wound was bad, and I spent several weeks under a heavy blanket of laudanum. By the time I was well enough to get out of bed, your note had already arrived."

Evangeline might well be feeling a sense of guilt over his injury, but he was shamed by the fact that he hadn't helped to ease her worry.

With the cloth removed once more, he picked up his shirt and slipped it over his head.

Under other circumstances, he would have been quite content to sit and enjoy his fiancée's ministrations. But they still had some way to go before nightfall.

Gus got to his feet and offered Evangeline his hand. She shook her head. "Rest your good arm. That's the one we might need if it comes to a gunfight."

She walked away, tossing the water out of the bucket. As she headed in the direction of the horses, he caught her words. "Fancy leaving your rifle behind. You stupid girl."

Her anger was understandable. Not only had she attacked their enemy, but without her rifle, she wouldn't be able to defend herself. Gus could only pray that her mistake was not going to cost them dearly.

As he picked up his jacket and coat, grimacing as he put them back on, he wrestled with a worrying thought. What if they were caught by the Lamballe gang—would he be able to protect her?

I will die trying.

Chapter Twenty-Eight

❧

They continued on the road, neither saying more than the odd word or two. Gus racked his brains, trying to conceive a way they could successfully make it safely to Binic. By the time another three hours had elapsed, he still didn't have a solid plan.

Every option Gus came up with and painstakingly deliberated was eventually cast aside due to one reason. There was every chance that Marec would have also thought of it. Their enemy was a formidable adversary.

We just have to keep heading toward the coast and hope that something or someone comes to our aid. Being ahead of them is our only advantage.

"Do you think your mother will like me, or will she consider me strange?"

Gus stirred from his musings and stared in surprise at Evangeline. She was riding alongside him on Gobain. And if her tightly knitted brow was any indication, she was genuinely concerned about the reception she would receive from the Jones family.

Where did that come from?

"My mother will welcome you with open arms. Why shouldn't she?" he replied.

"Well, for a start, I am not English. I am also a Catholic. And the moment she starts asking about my life here in France, she is going to quickly realize that I am no gently bred young miss."

Evangeline had clearly put some thought into her question. Had examined all the pros and cons of the situation. And if he was reading her mood right, she had probably come to the conclusion that Mrs. Jones would be horrified at her son's choice of wife.

With a tug of his horse's reins, Gus brought his mount to a halt. Evangeline did the same. He turned in the saddle and faced her. "I am one of seven children. Every single one of whom has made plenty of mistakes in their lives. Not that I am saying you are any sort of slip up. What I am saying is that to my knowledge, my mother has dealt with her children's life decisions in a calm and rational manner."

She frowned at his words. He clearly hadn't sold her on the devil-may-care attitude that his mother had adopted over the years. She was the wife of a naval officer; it was expected that she would deal with problems in a pragmatic way.

"Mama will love you. Any woman who takes on the role of trying to tame her wayward son will be top of her Christmas-gift list. You can count on that."

There were plenty of young ladies in London who had at one time or another thought themselves up to the task. However, once they got to know Gus beyond a quick hello, they had all abandoned their marriage campaigns. He may or may not have exaggerated some of his less pleasant habits in order to scare them off.

"What about money? And we will need somewhere to live. Have you considered that? And. And." She threw her hands up in the air.

Damn. She has got herself into a bit of a state over worrying about our future.

Gus did a quick check over his shoulder. There were no other travelers on the road. He nodded in the direction of a cluster of trees. From the lay of the land, it was obvious that a river ran parallel to the road. After long hours of travel, the horses could do with a drink. "Come on. Let's ride over there and let the horses take a rest. It's far enough from the road that we will be able to see anyone approaching."

She followed him to the water. "From memory, I think this is a small branch of the river Cré, which means we are still north of Lamballe. But at least we are getting closer to the sea."

Gus dismounted then waited for Evangeline to do the same. With a resigned huff, she finally threw her leg over the side of her saddle and slid to the ground.

Her landing was steady. There was no obvious sign of discomfort from her ankle.

Good. That means it is just a slight twinge, not a sprain.

While the horses wandered over to the stream and helped themselves, Gus turned his attention to Evangeline. "What is the real problem here? If it is money, I have plenty. I can sell the boat to buy a house or at least rent one if you wish. I can give up the smuggling. My father has been badgering me to go and work for the British admiralty ever since the war ended."

With Europe once more at peace, trade was high on the list of endeavors for the government. A man who knew the tides, winds, and English Channel, as well as Gus, was an asset to be utilized.

"But you are a smuggler at heart," she replied.

"That cannot last. I was also once a spy and an operative for His Majesty the King. Those assignments eventually came to an end. This business is getting more dangerous with every passing year. And then there are men like Vincent ready to do whatever they have to in order to push people like you and Armand out."

She screwed up her face. "It's not all his fault. We did provoke him."

There had been a small question in the back of Gus's mind as to why the Lamballe gang were so set against the La Roche family. Why had they attacked them? What might Armand have done to cause such enmity?

When Evangeline wouldn't meet his gaze, Gus took a deep breath and did his best to settle his temper.

Or was it, Evangeline?

"Evangeline, sweet girl, what did you and Armand do?"

Having spent a lifetime in the company of liars, Gus could read all the signs of when someone had decided to put their falsehoods aside and finally tell the truth. Her clasped hands and tight smile gave her away.

"Ah. How do I put this?"

"Plain and without a hint of embellishment would be good."

She offered him up another tentative smile, but Gus wasn't having any of it. He stared her down, determined that she would tell him.

Evangeline heaved a tired sigh. "The brandy you were trying to load on board your yacht during that last trip belonged to the Lamballe gang. Well—it should have. I intercepted the shipment on the road up from Rennes and made a fresh deal with the supplier. I paid him one franc more than Vincent was prepared to, along with the promise not to shoot him. It was an offer he couldn't refuse."

Little wonder Vincent attacked us when we were trying to move the brandy. We were lucky he didn't just shoot the whole crew of the Night Wind.

Any hope of his keeping his anger under control went straight out the window. "Bloody hell, Evangeline! You don't poke a bear with a stick! What were you and Armand thinking?"

They had fired the first shot in this war. Marec and his men were simply fighting back.

His blood rose to boiling point, but instead of looking contrite, Evangeline stuck her hands on her hips and glared at him.

"Are you quite finished?" she snapped.

Is she in jest?

He shook his head. He was far from done.

Lord give me the strength not to throttle this woman.

Gus didn't hold with violence against women. But that didn't mean Evangeline was going to escape his wrath. She was due for a thorough tongue-lashing. "Don't you understand the smugglers code? You don't undercut one another. Your common enemy is the customs men on both sides of the channel. They are who we are up against."

"We didn't start this; Vincent did. Since the end of the war, there has been a steady stream of former soldiers looking for work. Armand employed as many of them as he could. But when Vincent decided he wanted in on our part of the smuggling trade, things changed."

"I understand," he replied.

"No, you don't. You and your friends always treated Armand like he was some local dignitary. You fawned all over him. And it suited everyone. But what you don't know is that I am the one who has been running things. My uncle was the polite façade of our business. Or he was until he decided that Vincent had to be taught a lesson."

Gus flinched. He had always thought that Evangeline was somehow involved in the operations; he had never suspected she was the mastermind behind it all. His future wife was full of unpleasant surprises.

"Armand offered to go into business with Vincent and the Lamballe gang, and I was furious. No one was giving all my hard work away. And when Vincent refused, I was more than happy. I wanted him out of our lives. Then, of course, Armand got it into this head that his honor had been insulted, and he decided to fight."

She waved her arms in the air. "And then it all become one great big tourbillon."

A whirlwind of violence and retribution. One which they were standing right in the middle of, with no easy way out.

Now Gus understood the real reason for Evangeline's questions about his mother. He wasn't bringing a young, sweet woman home as his wife. His bride was a battle-hardened smuggler with a will of her own. Evangeline was worried that she wouldn't be able to live up to the expectations of London high society.

He came to her, slipping his arm around her waist. "If we live through the next few days, you and I are going to have some serious conversations about working together as partners. And that includes not starting any more blood feuds."

Evangeline rested her head against his chest. "Yes, I think I have learned my lesson on that point."

Gus kissed the top of her hair. He wanted a life with this woman. If they had to fight prejudice in order to make their marriage work, he was more than ready. Finding a place in London society where Evangeline could be herself was not going to be easy. "I am not promising anything, but when we get to England, I shall speak to Monsale. He might be able to find a use for your skills within the RR Coaching Company."

She lifted her head and gifted him with a smile. Her emerald-green eyes shone bright in the afternoon sun.

You are a beautiful woman, Evangeline. I can't wait to make you mine.

"Thank you. I would much rather be dealing with cargo and money than sitting in drawing rooms, drinking tea."

"Don't I know it." He captured her lips, pulling her hard against him as their tongues met in a heated embrace.

Chapter Twenty-Nine

The rest of the afternoon was spent slowly making their way along the back roads, following the path of the river. It was long and tiring, but as night drew close, Evangeline caught the first hint of sea air on the breeze. A small spark of hope lit in her heart.

If we could reach Binic, we might be able to make our escape.

They passed through a crossroad just as the sun was setting. She nodded at the stone marker, partially hidden in the grass. "The way ahead leads to the main road to Lamballe. If we turn west here, we should be able to get close to Saint-Brieuc and then go around it."

"I don't suppose there are any villages or hamlets between here and there?" replied Gus.

"No, nothing. We shall have to sleep under the stars tonight. There is, of course, the odd barn along the way. I am assuming you wouldn't want to stay in one of those as that would be the first place Vincent's men would look if they do happen to come along this road."

Gus gave a nod. "Smart thinking. Any sort of building will be a marked place. Vincent was a military man; he will know where to look. Safer for us to hide somewhere in the trees far from the road. The horses won't be seen."

She was quickly developing a liking for his smiles and small acknowledgements. He might be their notional leader, but Gus clearly considered her words to be of value whenever she offered an opinion.

It's nice to be listened to—not just sent into the kitchens to inquire about supper.

Armand had been happy to let Evangeline run the smuggling side of things, but at times hadn't fully acknowledged her contributions.

A short while later, Gus pointed to a clump of bushes away to the left. "That looks good. It's far enough that the horses won't be heard if they whiny or snort, but also near to the road if we have to make a sudden run for it."

When they had turned at the crossroads, they were still a good ten miles from Saint-Brieuc. Evangeline guessed they were probably now seven to eight miles from the town. Close enough, but still a long way from Binic.

If Vincent and his men did give chase, she and Gus would have few places they could go. A safe refuge seemed far away.

At the edge of the road, they both dismounted their horses. The grass was long and there were marshy patches, which proved difficult to navigate around. It took some effort to ensure that the horses did not step into any holes and injure themselves.

Finally, they reached a dry patch of ground, close to the riverbank. They settled behind the bushes, out of sight from the road. It wasn't the same comfort as the hotel in Dinan, but it was the best they could do.

Evangeline glanced up at the sky. "I hope the rain holds off for tonight. If it does, we might get some sleep."

Gus, who was busy retrieving food from his saddlebags,

merely nodded. He had been quiet for most of the time since they had resumed their ride. At times, she had ventured sideways glances at him, all the while trying to figure out what he was thinking. To gauge if he was still angry. Or if he was wondering how, he could make a life with her. His smuggler wife.

At least he knows it all now. Everything I have done and who I am.

No more secrets.

But would it be enough?

She held her breath as he approached, fearful that he might say something to confirm her worst fears. That he was still going to go through with the wedding, but that he was marrying a woman he truly didn't know.

"There is some bread and a small square of cheese. That's about all the food we have left," he said.

Unsure as to what she should say, Evangeline stayed silent.

Gus lifted his head and met her gaze. "Are you hungry?"

"You have it."

"Are you alright?"

"Yes, just worried about what is to come. I hadn't put much thought into my future, living for each day as it came. And there are things I should have said to Armand; things which will now be forever unsaid. You have also been quiet."

"Busy trying to come up with a plan that covers as many contingencies as possible. I'm worried that we haven't seen any sign of Marec and his men. They must know by now that we are not on the road to Paris."

Evangeline knew Vincent and the way he worked. Gus's fears were well grounded. The Lamballe gang could be deliberately lagging behind them in order to let her and Gus ride blindly into a trap. "It would help immensely if I could figure out exactly where we were. I know a few people in this area. Jodoc and his wife are not the only ones who have connections with my family," she replied.

THE ROGUE AND THE JEWEL

She didn't want to seek shelter with the locals, worried that it could cause trouble. What they needed was information. "If we were able to reach out to one of our friends, they might at least be able to share news of the Lamballe gang. I don't want to put anyone in danger, mind you. But knowing anything about where Vincent might be headed would help."

Gus broke the block of cheese in half and handed a piece to her. They sat on the ground while they finished the last of the food. By the time they were done, the sun had well and truly set.

The moon had shifted from full to a waning gibbous, but there was still enough light for them to be able to see one another clearly. And while the early spring night was chill, they dared not risk a fire. Even a small flame could send signals to anyone searching for them.

They huddled close, with Evangeline stuffing her hands into the large pockets of her father's coat to keep them warm. She had been in too great a hurry that morning at the château to remember to pack her gloves.

"Come closer. Let me keep you from the cold," said Gus.

He pulled off his hat and wig, setting the hair to one side. A grateful Evangeline took the hat and propped it under her head as she lay down. Gus snuggled up next to her on the ground.

"Did you know that your hair almost glows in the dark? You look like one of those religious paintings with a halo around your head," he said.

Evangeline grinned up at him. She couldn't ever recall having her hair likened to a nimbus before. "Do you think I look like the Venus de Milo and that I should be standing on a giant shell?"

He leaned over and brushed a kiss on her cheek. "The Venus de Milo is the statue without any arms. The painting to which you refer is Botticelli's Birth of Venus. And she had red hair."

A giggle escaped her lips. "So much for my education. My mother was always saying I spent too much time reading mathematics and not enough studying the Renaissance."

Gus cleared his throat. "Actually, I only know that because George Hawkins was considering stealing a Titian painting at one point. He studied up on Italian masters for a time. But enough about friends."

A second kiss found its way to her cheek. Gus's third kiss trailed down her neck. Evangeline shivered at his touch. Heat pooled between her legs.

"Tell me, my sweet, does the hair at the entrance to your sex also glow in the dark? I can't wait to see if it does," he whispered.

The sensation of his warm breath on her skin had Evangeline biting her bottom lip. "Not telling," she teased.

Gus groaned. "You torture me."

Evangeline's nimble fingers swiftly worked to release several of her buttons. She opened the bottom of her coat. Grabbing a hold of Gus's hand, she settled it on the hem of her gown. "You might not get to see tonight, but you most certainly can touch. If you like."

They were so close that she caught sight of his Adam's apple as it bobbed up and down when he swallowed. His breath came in short gasps. "May I?" he asked.

She bunched up her skirts, slowly lifting them. His fingers followed.

"Lie back for me," he commanded.

Her eyes closed as the tip of his thumb touched the outer folds of her sex. They opened as he pushed it deep into her wet heat and began to stroke. Evangeline groaned.

Gus nipped at her earlobe and murmured, "Shh, you must be quiet. Don't startle the horses."

He captured her next soft cry with his mouth, his tongue, and thumb working in concert with one another.

The pressure slowly built, but he wouldn't release her

from the kiss. He shifted his hand, slipping two fingers into her sex. His thumb rubbed over her sensitive bud. Gus had large hands, and his fingers stretched her tight sheath. It wasn't painful; it was divine.

Evangeline was on the verge of climax when she broke free of the kiss. "Do you want to be inside me when I come?"

He nodded. "More than anything. But not here. When I take you for the first time, it will be in a bed. And you will be my wife. Watching you, touching you is a heady mix of both pleasure and torture for me. My reward will be when you reach completion." His mouth came down on hers once more, and the pace of his strokes increased.

Evangeline lifted her hands and tightly gripped the brim on either side of Gus's hat.

She was so close now; her climax tantalizingly near.

In a flurry of movement, Gus tore his lips from hers. He shifted down her body. A gasp escaped her lips as he removed his fingers from her sex, only to then replace them with his wicked tongue. He sucked and licked her sensitive nib. Evangeline had just enough time to cover her mouth with her hand. She let out a muffled cry as her world suddenly shattered into a blinding orgasm.

Her climax continued to roll on as Gus worked his lips skillfully back and forth over her throbbing bud. A smile crept its way to her own lips. She couldn't wait for Gus to become master of their marital bedroom.

If she had to fight the entire Lamballe gang in order to make sure they got on that boat to England, she would.

Gus crawled over her and grinned. "I think your entire body is now glowing."

Chapter Thirty

※※※

Evangeline woke to a hand over her mouth. She was on the verge of screaming when she realized it was Gus who held her. He leaned in close and whispered, "Shh. There are horses on the road. I can hear men talking."

She sat up, peering through the bushes in the direction of where Gus pointed. There was no mistake—four horses were on the road. They were a good hundred yards away, but the riders were making no effort to speak softly.

"When I get into Saint-Brieuc, I am going to eat half a bloody horse."

"Bugger that. I will eat a whole one. I am starving."

The rider at the front of the group turned in his saddle. "You won't get a damn thing to eat until we catch up with that bitch and her fancy Englishman. So shut your mouths and keep your eyes peeled. They can't be far."

Gus rested his hand gently on Evangeline's shoulder. They both knew that voice. It was Vincent Marec. He and his men had rightly guessed that Evangeline and Gus had taken the back road to the coast.

They waited. Evangeline silently prayed to every saint she knew that the horses would stay quiet and not alert their pursuers. If she and Gus had to make a run for it, they would have to go across country. They wouldn't stand a chance out in the open.

It was a good ten minutes before Gus finally spoke. "Marec and his men are now ahead of us on the road. They only have to lay in wait to attack and overwhelm us. We must find a way to get to Binic without being seen."

The orange and yellow of sunrise was but a thin line on the horizon. Until she could see the surrounding area clearly, they couldn't risk moving from this spot.

"Come and rest. When it is light, I will do my best to figure out where we are. Then we can look to make a plan," she said.

She nodded in the direction of the horses. "The biggest problem we have is Gobain. There are not many horses like him in this area. Anyone who recognizes Gobain will know to whom he belongs."

They could alter direction and head north toward Jodoc's house, swapping their horses for his, but that would put them a good half-day behind. And possibly endanger their friends. The sooner they reached Binic, the better.

As they settled back to their sleeping places, Evangeline set her mind to work.

There has to be a way for us to get to the coast without being seen. But how?

༶

There was a weird noise coming from the left of him. Gus cracked open an eyelid and turned his head. Then he squealed like a frightened little child.

Not two feet away stood a huge black and white Pie Noir cow. Its curved horns filled his entire field of vision. He rolled over onto his bad side, winced, but kept going. He struggled to his feet.

"Where did you come from?"

He looked around. And more importantly, where was Evangeline?

His heart had been racing at a fair clip already at the sight of the cow, but Evangeline's absence sent it to a full gallop.

Without a moment's thought, he picked up his tricorne hat and put his hand inside. The lining was cold. The last time he had seen Evangeline, she had been resting her head on it. If she had only left to go down to the river and attend to her ablutions, it should still be warm.

Fear gripped him.

You had better not have gone off to do something brave and foolish.

He couldn't bear it if Evangeline had decided to sacrifice herself in order to save him.

Hurrying down to the river's edge, he quickly scanned the surroundings. Both horses were still there, happily nibbling on grass. She hadn't taken Gobain and dashed off somewhere. That was a small relief.

"Where are you?" he muttered.

Returning to the place they had slept; he encountered more cows. A dozen or so appeared to have found his saddlebags to be of great interest.

That's all I need—cow slobber on my things.

Waving his arms about, Gus shooed them away. As the herd parted, Evangeline appeared walking toward him. She pointed at one of the nearby beasts. "That one has your wig."

He glared at her, not giving a damn about the hairpiece. "Where have you been?" he demanded.

She reached his side then turned and pointed back in the direction from where she had come. "At Alain Rufus's house. This is his farm. In the fading light last night, I didn't recognize the place. And earlier, you were sleeping so soundly that it seemed a pity to wake you."

Evangeline stepped past him and bent to pick up his hat.

She offered it to Gus with a smile. "Vincent and his men stopped at Alain's house late last night. They were continuing on to Saint-Brieuc. We are safe for the time being."

She glanced at the cows. "I didn't think about the milking herd when I left. I'm sorry about your wig."

Gus snatched the hat out of her hands then stopped. He hated himself. Stealing her joy was the last thing he wanted. Evangeline had suffered enough over the past days.

"Is Alain to be trusted?"

She gave a firm nod. "He has worked closely with us over the years, and I can assure you that he has no love for Vincent or his gang."

He reached out and gently pulled her into his arms, placing a tender kiss on her lips. "I'm sorry I was angry. You scared me by leaving like that. Please don't do it again."

He dared not tell her that the past few minutes had been like living one of his worst nightmares. In London, while he had been under the influence of laudanum, his nights had been filled with angry, desperate dreams. Of holding a bloodied, wounded Evangeline in his arms as she lay dying.

Gus blinked back tears as a simple and undeniable truth settled in his mind.

I love her. I cannot imagine a life without this woman.

Evangeline met his gaze. The timid smile on her lips held the promise of forgiveness.

"Come and have some food. Alain's wife has made broth, and there are fresh eggs. After a large cup of coffee, I promise you will feel more human."

He accepted her kiss and whispered, "All I need is you."

"You will always have me, Gus Jones. Now come and eat."

Chapter Thirty-One

Harry and Stephen had always pressed upon Gus the need for a man to have friends. To know that in times of danger there were people that could be counted upon. Alain Rufus was one of those men.

Gus took in the cramped kitchen and dining space of the farmhouse. It was lovely and warm thanks to the fire blazing in the hearth against the far wall. The gray haired, shaggy-bearded farmer greeted him with a generous hug, then quickly offered him a seat at the large, battered old table. It reminded Gus of the one at the RR Coaching Company offices, and he felt a sudden pang of homesickness.

I wonder if the lads are thinking about me this morning.

He could just imagine what each one of them would say if they knew where he was and what a mess, he and Evangeline had got themselves into. Harry and George would no doubt congratulate him on having got this far, while Stephen would offer up carefully considered words of caution.

As for Monsale—he would demand to know where all the weapons were and how Gus planned to kill Vincent Marec. Then his attention would turn to how best the rogues of the road could capitalize on the situation and take over the French side of the smuggling operation.

Once a bloody-thirsty, thieving pirate, always . . .

Plans for the future could wait. All that mattered was finding a way to Binic. To seeing Evangeline safely on board the *Night Wind* and sailing for home.

Evangeline set a large bowl of fine chicken broth in front of him, along with a spoon. "This is good. I ate some while you were napping with the cows."

While Gus ate, Madame Rufus busied about the kitchen cooking eggs and giving Evangeline pointers about which herbs should go in a cassoulet. He was pleased to see that Evangeline paid close attention. He caught his fiancée's eye at one point, and she playfully poked the tip of her tongue out at him.

Minx. I can't wait to make you, my wife.

Alain drew up a chair and seated himself across the table from Gus. After pulling a pipe out of his jacket pocket, he proceeded to stuff it with tobacco.

In what was clearly a well-practiced move, he leaned back in the chair and selected a taper from a box by the fireside. He held it aloft. Without further ado, Madame Rufus shuffled over from her place at the stove, plucked the taper from her husband's fingers, lit it, and then handed it back to him. Alain blew his wife a kiss.

Gus grinned at the elegant ballet. It was one they had obviously danced together many times before. He appreciated the easy comfort of a long-married couple.

I hope Evangeline and I will be so blessed.

With his pipe lit, Alain rested his hands on the table and faced Gus. "Your horses are the problem, Augustus. So, I have come up with a solution."

"Yes?"

"I have been smuggling brandy and other tax-heavy items in my cart for a number of years. There is a long, shallow box at one end of the cart, much like an oversized coffin. Once I have it full of goods, I usually hide it under a pile of hay. It is not a sophisticated piece of deception, but it works."

Gus could see where this was leading. Hiding in a box was not something he had ever considered doing. One because he wasn't great with enclosed spaces, and two because he knew it was fraught with danger. It would be all too easy for someone to open the box and shoot whoever was hiding inside. "I am not sure about this, Alain."

I really don't want to spend any time in a box. Not while I am still alive.

Evangeline came to sit beside him. They exchanged a smile. She slipped her hand into his and gave a reassuring squeeze.

Gus began to struggle with his breathing, a sense of panic and fear slowing rising within him.

"If Vincent has gone on to Saint-Brieuc, we cannot openly travel on the road. The sea is not an option. This seems the best way," she said.

Alain took a deep drag on his pipe then blew the gray smoke into the air. "They are expecting Madame Rufus and I to be travelling on the road today. If we meet them, the Lamballe gang won't be suspicious."

Evangeline nodded. "They are heading up to Tréguidel with milk for the cheese makers at the abbey. The village is past Saint-Brieuc, not far from Binic."

While it was encouraging to hear them making plans, Gus still wasn't sold on the idea. So many things could go wrong.

And that box. Can I make it all that way?

"The brass milk pots do make a bit of noise as they clang together, but they will be full. The journey home is much worse. It's like riding with a cart full of bells," added Alain.

It all made sense. Hide in the cart. Get past the Lamballe gang. Make it to Binic and then escape. But the mere thought of being in the box had the broth churning in Gus's stomach.

Alain pointed at Gus's head. His brow was heavy with sweat.

"Is there a problem?"

Gus closed his eyes. Admitting his fear of small spaces wasn't something he was keen to do, but if he panicked in the box, it could well mean revealing Evangeline and his hiding place. His fear could kill them all. "I was stuck in one of my father's sea chests as a young boy. I spent over an hour in it. The air was stale, and I was on the verge of passing out when they found me." He was a grown man, had faced many dangers both during and since the war, yet nothing had come close to leaving the same mark on his psyche as being trapped in that metal box had done.

The gathering fell silent. He was weak. Shame crawled all over him.

"I can imagine how that would affect a young boy. Our minds are strange things. We experience something bad in our lives, and it never lets us go. Vincent's second in command, Claude, the one with the scarred face, he won't go near an open flame," replied Alain.

"I noticed he gave the torch a wide berth when he and Vincent were in the foyer of the château," said Evangeline.

"Claude is not a wicked man like his boss. I have offered him work here at the farm. I'm certain that it is only the fear of what Marec would do to him that stops Claude from walking away from the Lamballe gang."

Gus withdrew his hand from Evangeline's and got to his feet. With his wig gone, he had the luxury to run his fingers through his short hair. "Could we at least have the lid of the box partly off while we travel? If you see anyone up ahead, one of you could hum or whistle in warning."

"We would need something louder to be heard over the clanging of the pots. How about *La Marseillaise*? If we see anyone on the road, we can strike up the song," offered Madame Rufus.

Her husband clapped his hands together. "You are a clever woman."

The French national anthem was not something Gus had ever heard. And he could only hope that today wouldn't be the first time he did. "If it is the only option, then we can but try. Rather than stand here and worry about it, we should get on the road."

Evangeline got to her feet. "We appreciate the risk that the two of you are taking. If I don't get the opportunity to speak to you later, thank you. Alain, I hope you get a good price when you sell our horses. Madame Rufus, make sure he uses some of the proceeds to buy you a new gown and some fancy boots."

Madame Rufus grinned at her husband. "And a pretty bonnet to wear to church on Sunday."

Alain headed for the door. "The cart is almost loaded. We should be ready to leave soon."

Evangeline followed Gus out to the yard. When she touched him on the arm, he visibly flinched. Heat raced to his cheeks. "I feel such a fool over the worry of being in a box."

"We all have things we cannot control. Just remember, I will be with you the whole way," she said.

He swallowed down a lump of dread. "How far is it to Binic from here?"

"Roughly thirteen miles. At the speed of a horse and cart, it will take us a good three to four hours. I could teach you *La Marseillaise* while we are on the road. It would be a good distraction."

The broth and omelet churned once more in his gut.

Three to four hours. The devil should take me.

By the time they reached the seaport, he would be word-perfect with the song.

Chapter Thirty-Two

Evangeline's right hand eventually lost all feeling. Considering how hard Gus was squeezing it, she was rather relived. Her brave, fearless sailor lay beside her in the wooden box. He was as stiff as a corpse. The only signs that he was alive were the beads of sweat on his brow and his labored breathing.

For the first hour of their journey, she talked. Told him everything from her earliest childhood memories, including the years when the La Roche family had been forced to live away from their own home. She skipped the parts about the death of her parents, figuring that wouldn't help Gus in the current situation.

He managed the occasional grunt or nod, but no real conversation. She couldn't imagine what he was going through.

"And then we get to just after Napoleon had been exiled to the island of Elba, and the night Sir Stephen Moore and George Hawkins arrived at our doorstep in the middle of a storm."

Gus turned and gave her a grim smile. She was encouraged by this glimmer of life from him.

Good. Familiar stories might help.

"Go on," he whispered.

"That first time, Stephen was very businesslike. I expect he knew the danger that working together could put us all in. The British hadn't signed the Treaty of Fontainebleau, so we were still technically at war."

"Stephen was more concerned about the negotiations rather than ongoing arguments over Napoleon. He was nervous on the boat, kept worrying that his command of the French language wasn't good enough and your uncle would take offense," he replied.

Finding two pistol-brandishing Englishmen standing in the foyer of her family home had come as quite a surprise, though not as big a shock as when they'd announced that they were looking to form a smuggling alliance with Armand.

The memory of Armand brought tears to Evangeline's eyes. She was doing her best to hold back her grief, knowing that when it finally did hit her, the tears would be impossible to stop.

"And then you appeared the next morning." She would never forget the first time she laid eyes on the man who now held her heart. He had been walking up the hill from the small jetty with the sun at his back, the light through the trees creating a dappled effect all around him. It had been magical.

For a moment she had simply stood and stared, lost for words at the sight of this unusually clad stranger. His greatcoat and tricorne hat old-fashioned remnants of a past era, and that magnificent dark brown mane of his, stunning.

Evangeline reached over and pinched Gus.

"Ow. What was that for?" he said.

"For making me think your hair was real. I was so disappointed when you took off your hat and wig."

Evangeline was relieved when Gus laughed. They still had some way to go before they reached Binic. Anything which calmed him was welcome.

THE ROGUE AND THE JEWEL

"I should buy you . . ."

The first strains of *La Marseillaise* drifted to her ears, bringing their light banter to a sudden halt. Gus cocked his pistol and took a deep breath. The first person who opened the lid was going to be met with a loaded weapon pointed at them.

"I love you," she whispered.

Chapter Thirty-Three

Gus glanced over at Evangeline. The promise he had made to his father not to be a hero sprang immediately to mind. But if it meant keeping her safe, he would gladly sacrifice himself.

This woman means everything to me. Without her, life wouldn't be worth living.

"I love you too," he replied.

He reached for the edge of the lid and pulled it down. It dropped firmly into place. They were immediately plunged into darkness.

Gus silently cursed the skills of the craftsman who had built this box. There wasn't a crack of light. The air would soon turn stale.

He hoped that Alain and his wife would quickly charm their way into being allowed to continue on the road. Anything so that he could breathe fresh air again.

The cart came to a stop. "Bonjour, Vincent. Bonjour, Claude!" The Rufus's cheery greeting gave away the identity of those who had intercepted them.

"Bonjour," replied Claude.

Vincent was his usual gruff self and gave a loud snort. "Where are you off to this morning?"

"The same place we said last night. Tréguidel with milk for the cheese makers. You can see the pots are in the cart," replied Alain.

"Go check," ordered Vincent.

Wrapping his fingers around the wrist which held the gun, Gus steadied his hand. His heart was thumping hard in his chest.

The cart shifted from side to side. He could only hazard a guess that Alain had climbed down. Heavy boots on the road drew closer.

"See? Brass milk pots. Pick one up," offered Alain.

"Did you see anyone on the road this morning?" asked Claude.

"No. The road has been clear of other travelers. But we have been keeping an eye out for any sign of the La Roche girl."

"Yes, poor Evangeline. I cannot imagine what she must be going through. That English pig murdering her uncle and then kidnapping her. Alain has promised me that he will shoot that long-haired fiend on sight," added Madame Rufus.

Gus's heart was now pounding so hard, his ears throbbed. Fear and adrenaline coursed through his veins. It had been a long time since he had faced such a deadly situation.

Beside him, Evangeline was silent.

His pistol was ready to deliver death to the first of Vincent's men—the knife hidden beneath his coat destined for the next man foolish enough to peer into the box.

"What's in the case?" asked Claude.

"Bits and pieces. Rope and other things," replied Alain.

"Open it."

Gus held his breath.

There was a brief moment of silence, followed by the creak

of the wood as the lid of the box was lifted. Sunlight and fresh air rushed in.

He was still blinking when a badly scarred face appeared. Gus pointed the pistol right between the other man's eyes. The message was clear—*if I die, so do you*. Their gazes locked on one another for a split second.

"What's in there?" asked Vincent.

Claude moved his head around. Gus imagined that from a distance, it might appear as if he was checking its contents.

"Ropes, an old blanket, and a broken bridle." Claude let go of the lid, and it closed once more.

"Ah, yes. I have been meaning to get the tanner to fix that piece of leather," said Alain.

Evangeline's hand settled on the side of Gus's leg. He was too busy wondering what on earth had just happened to respond to her touch.

"Let's get going," yelled Vincent.

The cart moved once more as Alain climbed back on board. "Good luck in your search. I hope you find them."

"Godspeed," added Madame Rufus.

The muffled sound of hooves slowly faded away. Gus waited as long as he could—until the air in the box was hot and heavy—before finally daring to lift the lid. He shifted it open just a crack.

"What happened?" whispered Evangeline.

Gus didn't reply. He had no answer to her question. Claude had seen them. Could have easily killed them both, and yet he hadn't.

He lied to Vincent.

Recalling Alain's words about Vincent's second in charge, a surprising thought sprang to his mind.

There was dissention in the ranks of the Lamballe gang. If they could find a way to exploit it, they might stand a chance of overthrowing Vincent. The notion was a tempting one. Monsale would most certainly approve.

Don't be a fool. You have to get Evangeline out of the country. Let the French sort this out between themselves.

Rough fingers curved under the lid of the box, and it lifted fully open. Alain's friendly face appeared. "I told you Claude wasn't completely bad. It is a brave man who dares to lie to Marec."

Gus took in a long, deep lungful of the sweet, fresh air. He wanted nothing more than to sit up or even climb out of the cramped box, but he wasn't about to tempt the gods. He and Evangeline might well think they had been spared, but who was to say that Vincent was not waiting for them around the next corner?

Only a fool underestimated Vincent Marec.

"How much longer before we reach Binic? I don't want to sound ungrateful, but I would prefer we kept moving," he said.

"Yes, the sooner we make it the better. Then perhaps we will have time to figure out what Claude is up to," added Evangeline.

They jammed a blanket in the end of the box, allowing air and light to filter in through the other two sides, then loosely set the lid on top. At the first sign of trouble, Evangeline could pull the woolen cover free and let the top fall.

There was silence between them. Gus forced himself to focus on the worry of getting the *Night Wind* out of the harbor. He could well imagine Evangeline was pondering how she could use Claude to get even with Vincent. His fiancée, the master schemer.

Sometime later, she lifted her head and sniffed. "Salty air. We must be getting close to Binic."

When the first cry of a seabird reached his ears, Gus took a hold of Evangeline's hand. "I've never been so happy to hear the sound of a gull before in my entire life. That is the last time I ever curse one of them for stealing my bait."

They were going to make it.

Chapter Thirty-Four

The cart pulled into the rear yard of number 12 Rue Wilson and came to a halt. Alain's boots clattered on the stone paving as he jumped down. When Evangeline gave him an expectant look, Gus put a finger to his lips. Until Alain gave them the all-clear, they were to remain silent and hidden in the box.

They endured a long ten-minute wait before the lid finally drew back. The face which greeted him was one he had thought he may never see again.

"About bloody time," said Captain Grey.

He held out his hand and pulled Evangeline up and into a seated position. Gus shuffled back in the cramped space. He rubbed his legs, working out the pins and needles as he righted himself.

The simple joy of being able to see above the rim of the box had tears pricking his eyes. "That was the worst experience of my whole life. I never thought swimming ashore from a French fort in the middle of the night could be beaten, but I would undertake that any day over being entombed."

Evangeline leaned over and slapped him on the arm. "I

was with you the whole time. Are you saying my company was that bad?"

"I couldn't have made it without you, my love."

Captain Grey cleared his throat.

Steadying himself against the back of the cart, Gus got to his feet and climbed out. After carefully navigating his way between the milk pots, he climbed over the side and jumped. He staggered a couple of paces as he landed on unsteady legs.

Once he was able to stand properly, Gus helped Evangeline out of the cart and set her onto the ground. She wobbled, and he quickly put an arm around her waist.

"We did it. You are the bravest man I know for having gone through all that," she said.

Gus turned to the captain. "How soon could we sail?"

His plan was simple. Evangeline and himself would hurry to the church, get married, and leave France on the evening tide. He didn't want to linger in Binic one minute longer than necessary.

Captain Grey screwed up his face. "We cannot leave harbor until late. We've had problems with a crack in the main mast. Ever since we got into port, the crew have been working to fix it. They have tarred, wrapped, and painted it twice already. The final cable is being served and parceled right now. It will take another couple of hours at least before the work is finished."

No one in their right mind would attempt to cross the English Channel in a yacht with a partly repaired mast. The perils of the sea were greater than a hundred heavily armed smugglers.

Gus raised an eyebrow at Evangeline. "Which means, we have time if you are ready to go through with this."

"And what exactly is this?"

He bent and placed a soft kiss on her lips. "Get married. I want you to be Madame Jones when you set foot on the boat."

"What an excellent idea."

They bid a grateful goodbye to Alain and Madame Rufus who were keen to carry on with their journey to the abbey in Tréguidel.

Captain Grey waited with Gus and Evangeline until the milk cart had disappeared from sight. He pulled his cap from his head and bowed to Evangeline. "I am sorry about Armand. We heard of his passing not long after we arrived."

"Thank you," she replied.

News travelled fast. Which to Gus was a worry in itself.

"It would be wise if you stayed out of sight as much as possible before we sail this evening. Marec's men have put a rumor about town that Evangeline La Roche was kidnapped by an Englishman. There is even a ten-franc bounty on your head," said Captain Grey.

"Ten francs? I thought I was worth at least fifty," replied Gus.

"For that sort of money, I would turn you in myself," said Evangeline. Captain Grey shot a sly grin in her direction.

With the wig gone, and not wearing his tricorne hat, Gus could only hope he might be a little less recognizable to the locals.

Evangeline pointed to the back of the building. "What is this place?"

Captain Grey moved away. "Perhaps I should head back to the yacht and leave you two to talk."

Gus nodded. He was reluctant to have this conversation right now, but Evangeline deserved to know the truth of his past before she signed the marriage certificate. "Go to the boat, pick the crewman with the cleanest shirt, and quickly bring him with you to the cathedral of Notre-Dame de Bon-Voyage. We will need two witnesses for a wedding. In the meantime, I shall see if I can find a priest."

"Right." The captain ran for the street.

Gus took a hold of Evangeline's hand and drew her to

him. He was not about to lie to her and then stand in front of a priest and say his vows. Only the truth would do. "For obvious reasons I have kept a number of things from you. One of them being that while I was an agent for the British crown during the war between our countries, we used to use this place as a safe house. I've sailed the waters around these parts and Northern Spain for a long time."

Her eyes narrowed as she met his gaze. "How long did you watch the château before you decided that we were the right people to approach for a smuggling operation?"

This was going to require a delicate touch. "Quite some time."

"How long?" she pressed.

He sifted through his memories, trying to recall the exact time frame. "We had been settled on Château-de-La-Roche for about six months before we finally approached you. Before that, we watched the estate on and off for over a year."

"You spied on us."

If the mistrust which dripped from Evangeline's lips was any indication, she wasn't taking this at all well.

Do it. Just tell her everything. She won't forgive you if you keep it a secret.

"Stephen and George did the reconnaissance work on the land; I was the one checking the coast. I used to watch you, Evangeline. When you went down to the beach behind the château, I would be hiding in the low shrubs along the top of the cove. It made my day whenever you stepped out onto the sand and the wind tussled your beautiful brown hair."

In Gus's mind, his observation of Evangeline had always been quite romantic, but now it just sounded odd and more than a little unsettling. He screwed up his face, unsure of what else he should say, fearful of adding fuel to the flame. "Does it help if I say I am sorry?" he ventured.

"No. And at some point, I intend to punish you for it. But what we need right now is for you to organize a hasty wedding, and for me to find somewhere to change. My hair is in need of attention."

At the rear of the building, Gus retrieved a key from a hiding spot next to the door. "Number 12 Rue Martin is still used by a number of my friends when they come to France. While the landlady doesn't know its wartime history, she is smart enough not to ask questions. In return for a generous annual stipend, she keeps it clean and ready for sudden arrivals."

With the rest of the RR Coaching Company currently based in England, they were guaranteed to have the house to themselves. It was the perfect place for Gus and his new bride to hide out for several hours until the boat sailed. Time which he intended to put to good use.

Chapter Thirty-Five

While Gus went to church in the hope of finding a priest to marry them, Evangeline took the opportunity to spend some time alone in the master bedroom of number 12 Rue Martin.

The pitcher of warm water and assortment of clean cloths the landlady had left felt heaven sent. She scrubbed the dust and sweat of the past days from her body before changing into her only remaining clean gown. After brushing her hair, she worked it into a braid.

"Not exactly how I expected to be wed, but it will have to do."

God willing, she would shortly be Gus's wife, and that was all that mattered. Once they were on board the *Night Wind* and on their way to England, then she could start to concern herself with planning her new life. One with the Jones family.

"I just hope his mother likes me."

After her clothes and hair were set to right, Evangeline spent a few minutes in silent prayer for Armand. Her uncle had wanted her to go with Gus to England, and she was happy that his wish was soon to be fulfilled.

Evangeline was seated on the bed, hands gently clasped together, ready to take the next step in her life, when a knock came at the door a short time later. She rose and, after confirming it was Gus, turned the key in the lock.

He rushed into the room, bringing an air of haste and excitement with him. "Monseigneur Baudet says he can't marry us. Under the Napoleonic code, we need a civil marriage license first. And since you don't live in Binic, it's impossible at such short notice."

His words spilled out at a rapid rate before he caught himself and slowed down.

"Sorry. I ran all the way here, and I . . . well, to be honest, I'm just a bit flustered. It's not every day that you attempt to get married—while at the same time trying to avoid getting murdered by a madman—only to be told no."

"Of course, we can't marry in Binic. It's outside my district. It hadn't crossed my mind," she replied. Her hopes for a wedding in France were suddenly dashed.

Gus took her face in his hands. "I promise once we are in London, we shall have a proper service and a celebration. You will get to meet all my friends and family. We will be married."

"If we cannot have a wedding, then what about the vigil for Armand? Could we do that?" she asked.

"The Monseigneur has agreed to hold a candle service for him later tonight, but unfortunately, we won't be here. Once the tide has turned and the *Night Wind* is ready to sail, we must leave."

Risking their lives in order to hold a vigil would be reckless and selfish. Armand's sacrifice did not deserve to be diminished by them dying. She placed a hand over her heart.

"I am disappointed with not being able to go to the church, but I understand. And besides, Armand, along with my parents, is here inside of me, and that's what counts."

It wasn't the time to worry about when or where they

would marry. But, with a civil wedding and a religious one now out of the question, they still had several hours to fill before the *Night Wind* put to sea.

It gave her an idea. "We might not be able to legally marry this afternoon, but we could still speak our vows. And for that, we only need us."

His gaze shifted to the bed and back to Evangeline "And then what?"

She licked her lips and smiled at him. "I'm sure we could think of something."

Chapter Thirty-Six

Evangeline untied the fine ribbon which held her braid together, slipping it from her hair. While Gus watched, a perplexed look on his face, she wound the ribbon around her ring finger, then tied it.

Holding it out for his inspection, she announced, "There. That should do."

"Is that what I think it is?"

Evangeline nodded at the emerald-and-gold striped ribbon. "Yes. It's my wedding ring. It is the symbol of our bond."

A grinning Gus wrapped his arms around her waist and drew Evangeline into his embrace. "I am going to have a long list of things to do once we get to England. Selecting a gold wedding ring will be at the very top."

She glanced at the simple band. "I don't need gold. Most women around here only have a plain copper ring. I expect it is the same for many brides in England. When the time comes, that will also be enough for me. Being your wife is more important."

He growled. "Are you defying me already? Evangeline Jones, you shall have a gold ring. As your husband, it is my right to gift you one."

His playful rebuke went straight to her heart. Gus already considered her his wife.

"I know you said we wouldn't become one in the biblical sense until we were wed. But I want our marriage to begin here in France. That way we will always have this place as a part of our lives," she said.

"I think that is a splendid idea." He quickly removed his coat and brushed a hand over his hair. Then taking her hand in his, he raised it to his lips and placed a kiss on the band of ribbon. "You might need to go first, because I'm not certain of the vows that you speak in church or even the ones we use in England. I don't make a habit of attending weddings."

Evangeline cleared her throat. "I, Evangeline Bijoux La Roche, do hereby take you, Augustus Trajan Jones, to be my husband. For richer, for poorer. In sickness and in health. Forsaking all others. Till death us do part. I swear this vow before God."

It wasn't perfect, but it was from her heart.

Gus chuckled. "You left out the obey bit."

She narrowed her eyes at him. When they managed to finally marry in front of a priest, she would be forced to say the word, but until then . . .

"And I, Augustus Trajan Jones, do hereby take you, Evangeline. Is Bijoux really your middle name? Doesn't that mean jewel in French?"

She might well be a widow very soon if he kept this up.

Your wicked grin is the only thing which might save you.

"I, Augustus Trajan Jones, do hereby take you, Evangeline Bijoux La Roche, to be my wife. For richer, for poorer. In sickness and in health. Forsaking all others. Till death us do part. I swear this vow before God."

Evangeline made the sign of the cross, and it was done.

"Now may I kiss the bride?"

"Please."

Gus bent and placed a tender, almost chaste kiss on Evangeline's lips. They might not be in church, but her new husband had clearly decided their first embrace as a married couple should be a socially acceptable one.

She wasn't having any of it.

As he drew back, she grasped the front of his jacket with both hands and held tight. They might have forgotten the *to have and to hold* part of the vows, but she was determined she would never let this man go.

"Now kiss your wife properly," she said.

Evangeline loosened her grip as Gus bent his head. She held her breath, ready for the moment when he would claim her mouth.

Strong hands settled about her waist and spun her around. Her back was to him. Gus blew gently in her ear. "Since I am your husband, I believe I am the one in charge, Madame Jones."

A shiver ran down her spine at hearing his heated words. Anticipation of what he might have in mind had lust, needy and hungry, coursing through her body.

She closed her eyes as Gus worked the rest of her braids free. He gave an appreciative groan as her long brown locks tumbled out. The end of her hair sat just above her waist.

"Perfect. When you are naked, I will get to see both your chocolate colored mane and that deliciously rounded arse."

She chortled. No one had ever spoken to her in such a lascivious and wicked way.

"Stay where you are," he instructed.

Boots clumped to the floor. Out of the corner of her eye, she caught a glimpse of a cravat being tossed onto a nearby chair. Jacket, shirt, and trousers quickly followed.

Hands appeared at her sides once more, bunching and lifting the hem of her gown.

"Time is of the essence today, but when we get to England

and have longer afternoons to indulge, I plan to do this *doucement*," he murmured.

And repeatedly, please.

He slipped her gown over her head. Evangeline was now clad only in her short stays, stockings, and boots. She reached for her laces and received an admonishing 'tsk' for her troubles.

"That's my job. I must voice my appreciation of the French mode of dress. None of those long stays and tight corsets. Once we are in London, you must engage the services of a modiste who can continue to dress you in such a way."

"You don't like the look of English ladies' undergarments?"

"Too much work to get them off."

After removing her boots and stockings, Gus set to work on her stays. As soon as they were open, Evangeline slipped them off.

A moment of shyness had her placing a hand over her naked breasts and turning her back to him once more.

"Trust me," Gus murmured.

A kiss was placed in the middle of her spine, followed by another. All the way to the top of her ass.

His fingers brushed over the soft skin of her rump.

"I am sorely tempted to take a bite," he murmured.

While she was still getting over the shock of his suggestion, it occurred to Evangeline that Gus was fully in command.

And that wouldn't do.

She took a deep breath and turned.

A wicked chuckle rose up from the man on the floor in front of her. He brushed his fingers over the short hair which covered her sex. "You are a goddess. I am such a fortunate man."

Her intention had been to make him stand, so she could

see him, but the moment Gus's tongue touched her heated core, Evangeline lost all sense and reason.

He delved deep, then traced a long lick from inside her all the way up to her sensitive bud, where he finished with a flourish.

"Oh. I. You. Oh. Gus," she babbled.

There was no escape. He set to the task with dedication and fervor, leaving her a quivering mess. Her knees were shaking by the time he finally sat on his haunches and grinned up at her.

Her gaze settled on Gus's manhood as he got to his feet. It was long and thick. Her fingers itched to touch it. "May I?" she asked.

"Of course. I am yours. You have full rights to this body."

She wrapped her fingers around the length of his erection, brushing her thumb over the head. The skin was pink and fine. "What should I do?"

Gus placed his hand over hers. "When we have time, I shall teach you. You will learn all you wish to know about pleasure, my love. How to give it and how to receive. But right now, I don't think I can hold out much longer. I need to have you."

The longing in his voice brought Evangeline to the verge of tears.

After arranging her on the bed, Gus crawled over Evangeline and settled between her legs. Their gazes met. She was held enraptured by his dark, stormy eyes. Lust shone in them.

"Take me, make me yours," she said.

As Gus's solid and thick erection slipped into her wet heat, Evangeline groaned. "Yes."

Chapter Thirty-Seven

Gus was tempted to remain in bed with Evangeline. With a naked, sated, and smiling wife beside him, he doubted few men would argue.

But leave they must. They had spent as long as they dared in the town. If Vincent was as wily as he appeared, there was every chance that he had men watching the *Night Wind*. Once Captain Grey and the crew started making sudden and hurried preparations to sail, the gang boss would soon hear about it.

Rolling over onto his side, Gus placed a soft kiss on his bride's lips. "Come, my love, we have to dress. The tide will be turning within the hour, and we need to get on board the boat."

"Can't we stay? I am sure the tide will be there tomorrow," she whined.

He kissed her once more before taking the blankets firmly in hand and throwing them back. Evangeline gave him a filthy look but climbed out of bed.

While she sat on the mattress, leisurely putting on her stockings, Gus quickly dressed. He pulled his hat on, arranging it into place. "This might well be the last time I wear this disguise," he said.

If he was going home to England, and giving up the smuggling trade, he wouldn't be needing a wig and tricorne hat anymore.

She rose and came around to his side of the bed. Evangeline pointed at the hat. "We could use it to play smuggler and bounty when we are alone in our bedroom. You could be the contraband, and I could steal you. I shall buy you a new wig as a wedding gift."

His manhood twitched. He could almost imagine it having a voice begging him to take her back to bed and have his way with her a third time.

But the yacht and crew were waiting. They had stayed in port long enough; he wouldn't win any friends if they missed the evening tide. "Alright, but then I get to play the head of the customs militia. I have some very unusual forms of punishment planned."

Her eyes grew wide at his teasing words. Rising up on her toes, she offered him her mouth. They shared a long, languid kiss.

"I can just imagine. And I promise to deserve them all," she whispered.

※

Hand in hand, they left the safe house and made their way along Rue Wilson to the dock. At the sight of the yacht, Evangeline's heart rate kicked up a notch. Her mouth grew dry.

She was really leaving France.

When she glanced at Gus, he turned and gave her a reassuring smile. It said all she needed to hear.

All will be well. We have a future together. Some day you will return.

Gus's footsteps slowed as they neared the boat. He

slipped his hand into his coat pocket and withdrew his pistol. He cocked it. "Something's not right."

Evangeline checked the weather deck. There was not a sailor to be seen. The sails were only partly set. If the *Night Wind* was going to sail with the tide, there should have been all hands on deck making ready.

Gus leaned over. "I want you to go back to the safe house. Wait for me there. If I don't come, you find your way to the church and seek sanctuary."

There was movement on the deck, and Captain Grey appeared. Behind him was Claude. Marec's number-two man held a pistol to the Englishman's head.

Evangeline made a move, doing as Gus had instructed. She had only gone a yard or so before she spied Vincent stepping out from a nearby doorway. He held a rifle, aimed squarely at her.

My rifle.

"Did you let him take his time with you, my dear, sweet Evangeline? Nice and gentle? Or did you fight him like you did me?"

She made slow steps back to her husband's side. Gus had his pistol lowered, his gaze moving back and forth between the two men. From the expression on his face, it was clear he was weighing up the situation.

Whichever of the gang you shoot first will leave the other open to kill.

Either way someone was sure to die.

As Vincent approached, other members of his gang fell in behind him. It was now five weapons against Gus's one.

"Move!" Vincent ordered.

Evangeline and Gus drew closer to the boat. When they neared the end of the gangplank, Vincent hurried and came to stand in front of them. "That will do, thank you."

A trickle of sweat slid down Evangeline's spine. She kept

her gaze on the rifle, her stomach dropping when Vincent aimed it at Gus.

No. Anyone but him. I couldn't bear to see my own weapon take my husband's life.

"Please, Vincent. If you have to kill someone today, then make it me. Gus has nothing to do with our fight. Let him and the crew of the yacht go. They are all innocents."

Vincent snorted. "And when did I ever listen to the words of a whore?"

"Evangeline is my wife," said Gus, his voice laced with menace.

There was an audible gasp from the men who had come with Vincent. Insulting a man's family in such a way clearly didn't sit well with them.

Claude pushed Captain Grey forward, following him off the yacht and onto dry land. "I thought you said she had been giving her favors to all the men on the estate. Now it turns out she is married," said Claude.

"And what happened to her being kidnapped?" asked another member of the gang.

Evangeline sensed a crack in the united front of Vincent's men. "We will leave France and never return. You can have what is left of Château-de-La-Roche. My cousin, Louis, will not likely want it. Along with that, you now have the smuggling trade you took from us. All of this will make killing my husband pointless," she said.

"Your husband was an enemy agent during the war. He worked against our country. As did you and your family," Vincent sneered.

She shook her head. "We were smugglers. Forced into it after we had our home and livelihood taken from us. We only ever shifted contraband such as brandy and English lace. None of my family were traitors. That's why Armand offered to work with you. He knew what it was to lose everything."

Out of the corner of her eye, Evangeline caught the look on Claude's face.

"Vincent, you never said anything about the old man offering to work with us. You said he was a stubborn fool who had told you we could all go to the devil."

Evangeline fought back tears. She had never understood Vincent's reasons for refusing such an offer. If she was going to die, then at least it would be with the truth finally out in the open. Turning from Vincent, she faced his men.

Armand, though your voice is now silent, I will speak for you.

"My uncle knew how hard life had been for you all since the end of the war. That many of you had sustained injuries that would never see you able to secure gainful employment. He wasn't a saint, but he didn't do what Vincent says he did."

The click of a rifle being cocked had Evangeline swallowing deeply. Any moment now she fully expected Vincent to train the weapon back on her and fire.

"What about how he blew the château up? He grabbed the torch and set it to the gunpowder," said Vincent.

"But we were the ones who brought a lit flame into his home. You were going to threaten to burn his house down," replied Claude.

"Shut up!" bellowed Vincent.

Evangeline turned her head, catching Gus's gaze. He was standing still, wisely letting Vincent and Claude battle it out.

To her surprise, Vincent lowered the rifle. He pointed a finger in her direction. "That scheming *salope* conned us out of our last shipment of brandy. Then she burned the stuff we had to buy to replace it. And she destroyed my farmhouse. Don't defend her!"

"I am not defending her. But don't you think there has been enough senseless destruction and death already? All of us are tired of constant battle. The war is over, and yet we are still fighting," replied Claude.

A distinct murmur of approval rippled through the Lamballe gang. Vincent was losing the argument.

Agitated, he lifted the rifle and aimed it at Gus's chest—at his heart. "Once this Englishman is dead, his widowed bitch will come with me. I am in charge, and I will be the one who decides when there has been enough blood . . ."

The rest of his manic speech fell to the ground, along with Vincent's lifeless body.

Evangeline gasped. Claude lowered his pistol and faced the rest of the gang. "If there is any one of you who disagrees with what I just did, feel free to put a shot in me. But if you want to live a better life, then you might just want to listen to my proposal."

As Claude stepped forward, Captain Grey quickly raced back up the gangplank and along the deck. He lifted the hatch which covered the stairs leading to the lower deck. Within seconds, the rest of the *Night Wind's* crew appeared.

Gus held up his hand, signaling for them to stay on board. Evangeline moved to his side, slipping her fingers into his. Her husband gave her hand a gentle squeeze. They were not out of the woods yet, but they had hope.

To her surprise, Claude didn't address Gus. Instead, his gaze settled on her. "The smuggling operation which has been run out of Château-de-La-Roche has a reputation for being one of the best. That is why Vincent wanted to take it. But I think he forgot that a major part of its success has always been the people behind it."

Evangeline blinked back tears. It was cold comfort to know that someone had seen the value that she and her uncle had contributed. If only Armand had been able to convince Vincent of that not-so-insignificant fact. But none of it mattered anymore.

"Armand is dead. And I am going to live in England. You are welcome to the ruins of the château," she replied.

"Why not stay? Come back to the château. Continue

running the smuggling trade. The Lamballe gang can provide the labor to rebuild the house and also help with the cargo," said Claude.

"And in return?" asked Gus. There was an unmistakable note of distrust in his voice. These men had been threatening the La Roche family for months.

Gus would never fully recover from the injury he had sustained at their hands. The fact that Vincent was dead, didn't wipe the slate clean.

Claude offered his pistol to Evangeline. She hesitated. This weapon had likely been used against her in the battle at the jetty. It was probably the same gun which had almost killed the man she loved.

With a tired sigh, Claude uncocked his pistol then tossed it on the ground. "My men need a home and a fresh start. They came back from years of war to nothing. For my injuries I received a letter of discharge and twenty francs."

Gus slowly nodded. "The English soldiers got pretty much the same treatment. Many are leaving for the colonies; the rest have to fend for themselves. So much for our grateful nations. The ordinary man pays the price for the machinations of kings and emperors."

These men had much in common. They had gone to war against one another, but with peace, they now faced the question of how they should move on with their lives. And rebuild.

It was over; Evangeline swayed unsteadily on her feet as the realization hit her. Relief now battled with the unexpected offer to remain in France. Only a minute ago, she had thought herself about to die. Now she was faced with a monumental decision.

Perhaps we could make this work. But what about Gus?

"Claude, could you please give my husband and me just a moment to talk?"

She wanted nothing more than to go home and pick up

the pieces of her old life. But it was no longer just her that she had to consider. Gus was the other half of her whole.

Gus held out his hand. "Let's walk."

Chapter Thirty-Eight

A gun being shoved in his face and the thought of his imminent death was something Gus Jones had come somewhat to terms with over the past few days. What he hadn't remotely considered was the prospect of Vincent's men turning on their leader and killing him.

As he and Evangeline walked away from the gathering, Gus glanced over his shoulder. Vincent Marec still lay where he had fallen.

This is real.

They had put a good fifty yards between them and everyone else on the dockside when Evangeline slipped her hand from his and came to a sudden halt. Alone, she walked to the water's edge.

"Gus, I am sorely tempted by Claude's offer. It would mean the world to me to be able to stay here. To raise our children in France."

She spun on her heel and faced him.

"Which is why you should be the one to make the decision. I cannot think clearly enough. My heart is demanding to rule my head."

"If I said we should get on the boat and leave, would you, do it?" he replied.

Evangeline drew in a shaky breath and nodded. The tears which shone in her eyes sent daggers straight to his heart.

"Yes. I love you, Gus Jones. I would go anywhere as long as we are together. This is the land of my birth, but my home is with you."

Tears pricked at his own eyes. Her words humbled him. It would break her heart to leave France, but for him, she would.

"And what if we stayed? If you took full charge of negotiating the cargos, while I continued to shift them across the Channel. Claude could focus on rebuilding the château as well as converting parts of the estate into small plots of housing for his men."

It wouldn't be easy. They would have to learn to work together for trust to be gained. But everyone stood to benefit if they could make it a success.

"I can write to Louis and offer to buy Château-de-La-Roche from him."

She raised an eyebrow. "Do you have access to that sort of money? Louis will still want a fair price, ruined house or not."

The contents of his flee box would be more than sufficient to pay out Evangeline's cousin. "Smuggling is a lucrative endeavor if one doesn't waste the profits. Where do you think the money for the *Night Wind* came from? So, in answer to your question, yes we will have money to become full owners."

He held out his arms to her, and Evangeline stepped into his embrace. A tender, loving kiss her reward.

"You would give up England for me?" she asked.

Gus grinned. "Yes, but the truth is my sacrifice would not be that big. I will still have to travel back and forth at times. You could even come with me."

A base in Brittany, along with the freedom to visit his family in London, was the perfect solution. They could have their cake and eat it too.

"I would love to meet your family. Though I am still terrified what your mother will think of me, especially if I take you away to live in France," she replied.

"Mama will just have to visit. We may need to hide some of the contraband while she is here, but I am sure we will be able to manage." He leaned in and met her gaze. "Evangeline, my love, say yes."

She grinned up at him. "If you are going to live in France, you had better embrace the language. So, my answer is *oui*."

※

After returning to the safe house, Gus and Evangeline quickly penned several letters. One was to Captain and Mrs. Jones informing them of their son's decision to remain in France, along with the first of what they imagined would be many invitations for them to visit Château-de-La-Roche.

The second was addressed to the Duke of Monsale in his capacity as chairman of the RR Coaching Company. It was an official letter notifying the board that Mister Augustus Trajan Jones was now going to be a director at large, effective immediately. Gus smirked at the thought of what Monsale would say when he opened the letter.

When the *Night Wind* sailed for England later that evening, both letters were safely in Captain Grey's keeping.

From the shore, Gus and Evangeline waved them a fond farewell.

"Well, this has been a day of surprises," she said.

"You can say that again. This morning I woke up in the middle of a field to the rather disturbing sight of a cow chewing on my wig. Tonight . . ."

"Tonight, you will be sleeping in a comfortable bed, with your wife in your arms."

He pulled her closer. It would take a little time to get used to the idea of them being a couple, of the changes in their lives. Gus found himself looking forward to it. To quiet moments alone with Evangeline, and to her, eventually finding peace.

Armand was gone, and that was a hole in her life, which only time could heal. Gus was determined to be there for Evangeline, for those moments when the cold reality of losing her uncle would catch her unawares. Her future happiness depended on him being able to shoulder some of the burden of grief.

As soon as they could arrange it, they would obtain a civil marriage license. In the summer, they would travel to England and have a wedding in front of family and friends. Monsale's inability to visit France compelled them to forgo a church service in Saint-Brieuc.

"I suggest we stay in Binic for tonight. We can go back to Saint-Brieuc and deal with things after tomorrow. What do you think?" he said.

Evangeline nodded. "My vote is for a fish supper from one of the cafés along the waterfront. And a bottle of muscadet. It would be good for the both of us to pause for a moment before going home. We have to bury Armand and then face the ruins of the château. The weeks ahead are going to be difficult."

"*Oui.*"

Evangeline softly smiled. "I will make a Frenchman of you yet."

Gus lifted his good arm and gave a final wave to the departing yacht as it rounded the head of the harbor and headed out to sea. It was odd to watch his own boat leave without him.

This is not adieu; this is simply au revoir.

Evangeline was right. They should take this precious moment together. There would be plenty of time in the future for them to make plans and to grieve the loss of Armand.

Tonight, he wanted it to be about them. To make love to his wife, and sleep with her safely curled beside him.

Epilogue

※

The moment her bare feet touched the soft sand, Evangeline's heart soared. For a time, she had thought this place lost. Gus had given it back to her.

Skirts held up, she continued on toward the water, gasping as the cold sea of the English Channel reached out and tickled her toes.

"I can't believe you are going bare foot into the sea. It must be freezing."

She turned and gave her husband a cheeky grin. It was cold, but she wasn't going to let on. If Gus had any idea as to how icy the water was, he would never venture past the edge of the sand.

"Come on in. The water is fine. It is good for you," she replied.

He shook his head. "Liar. I think sometimes you forget that you married a sailor. I know how bitterly cold the English Channel is on both sides. Just because we are in France, doesn't mean it is any warmer."

She lifted her gaze to the night sky, taking in the hundreds of stars which twinkled in a wide arch overhead. It was almost as if the hand of an ancient deity had tossed diamonds into the black, inky heavens.

My home. I love it here.

Profuse swearing had her shifting her attention from the gods to the mortal who had come to stand alongside her.

"I told you it was cold," he whined.

She stifled a laugh, but a guffaw escaped.

Gus playfully grabbed a hold of Evangeline, wrapping his arms around her. "Naughty minx," he admonished.

Evangeline snuggled in, resting her head against Gus's chest. She relished the comfortable ease of their love.

His scent was a heady mixture of sea salt and manliness. She would never get enough of it. Life was good. Every day a new beginning.

Claude and his men had been true to their word. The château was slowly being rebuilt. It was a smaller version of its original form, allowing for the extra stonework and bricks to be repurposed into building houses for the men from Lamballe.

Compromise on everyone's part had seen the estate around the château begin to flourish. There were plans to plant crops and raise livestock. The intent being to create a future for the people of the estate that wouldn't rely solely on illicit trade.

"I meant to ask you something. Claude and a couple of the other men wanted to know if they could start using the sea chapel for Sunday services. I told him I would speak to you," said Gus.

It was pleasing that they respected her family's heritage. And they deferred to Gus when there were particularly sticky questions. It hadn't taken long for him to become their leader. Claude had never wanted the role, being more than happy to lay bricks and till the earth.

"Absolutely. I think it a lovely idea. It will bring us all

together at least once a week and give the château back its heart."

He frowned at her. "What makes you think this place ever lost its soul? Evangeline, my love, you have always been the beating heart of Château-de-La-Roche."

She smiled at his sweet words. "Go on."

He pointed up at the sky. "Brighter than all that shines above."

"And what else?"

"More? Really? Let me see. A love that is precious beyond words. No. Ah! I have it. Your second name is Bijoux, so that makes you the jewel of Château-de-La-Roche."

Evangeline laughed. "I see we are going to have to work on your platitudes, Monsieur Jones. But I am happy to accept the title of being your jewel."

Yes, life was good and full of hope for the rogue and the jewel.

Monsale and Lady Naomi finally get their story.
King of Rogues

To win, they will both have to lose.
He has escaped the clutches of bloodthirsty pirates. Even managed to evade the entire French navy. But Andrew McNeal, the Duke of Monsale, may have finally run out of places to hide.
Duke's daughter, Lady Naomi Steele, has long had her marital sights set on the aristocratic leader of the Rogues of the Road.
When an ancient law is suddenly invoked, an unwilling Monsale is forced onto the marriage market.
He recruits Lady Naomi's mother to help him put together a list of potential wives.
Furious, Naomi refuses to be on the list. As far as she is

concerned, there should only be one woman Monsale is considering making his bride.
And when the stubborn, sexy rogue won't admit his mistake, Naomi decides to take matters into her own hands.
So, begins a steamy, high stakes game where the cards are marked, and hearts are wagered.
But who will fold first?

Turn the page to read the first chapter of
King of Rogues

Join my VIP readers and claim your FREE BOOK
A Wild English Rose

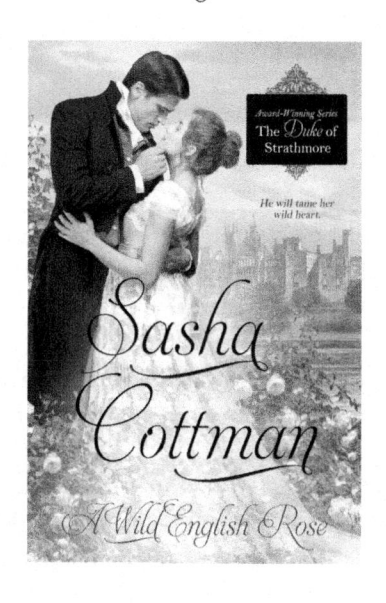

King of Rogues

July 1817
A private party
London, England

"Happy birthday Monsale. Thirty-three today, you poor old thing," said Harry.

"Not old, and most definitely not poor," snorted Monsale.

Lady Naomi Steele stifled a laugh. Her brother Harry was always giving Monsale grief over the fact that he was older than the other members of the RR Coaching Company. But Monsale had the right of it when it came to wealth. Of all the rogues of the road, he was by far and away the richest.

And the only one still unwed.

The three of them were standing to one side of an overcrowded ballroom in an elegant mansion in Duke Street. And while Harry and Monsale were each nursing a large brandy, Naomi was doing her best to appear casually interested in watching a dull quadrille that was taking place. She wasn't in the mood for champagne.

Harry's wife Alice had cried off from tonight's festivities. The exhausted new mother was at home getting some well-deserved sleep. A reluctant Naomi had been pestered into accompanying her brother this evening. Considering his former reputation as a society peacock, she thought it rather quaint that Harry had developed an aversion to attending social functions on his own.

The joy of being one half of a couple, I suppose.

Naomi turned and smiled at Monsale. "Yes, your grace, happy birthday, I wish you both health and happiness. And since your family is renowned for its longevity, I expect we shall have your company for many years to come."

Monsale raised an eyebrow. "Yes, well, only those family members who managed to avoid getting a stray bullet or a sword in their bellies were the ones graced with long lives. Fortunately, if my present run of luck holds, I should be able to look forward to making it to a ripe old age." He glanced down at his brandy glass, studying it for a moment. "It's the happiness bit I am not so certain of Lady Naomi— that appears to have eluded me."

Yes, well, a stone heart doesn't receive warmth, your grace.

Biting her tongue, Naomi turned her attention back to the dance. She would not be the one to make mention that a man could find happiness in the state of wedded bless.

I am willing to give you all my love for the rest of my life, Monsale. You simply have to ask.

Her generous offer did, however, come with some conditions. Monsale had to reciprocate her affections. To willingly offer up his own heart.

Naomi wouldn't ever enter into a loveless union. As far as she was concerned, spinsterhood was a far better option than being bound to a man who kept himself closed off from his wife's love.

Harry elbowed his friend in the ribs. "What you need to get yourself is a bride. A loving wife would bring you much joy. I can't believe I am saying this, but marriage has a great deal to offer a chap."

Lord Harry Steele had turned in his wicked party man card and become a dutiful husband and doting father. Naomi chanced a look at her brother, he was positively beaming. She had never seen him so happy. Love looked good on him.

If only she could say the same for herself. Unrequited love was a cruel burden at the best of times, at the worst— soul-destroying. Standing this close to the man who held her love so thoughtlessly in his hands had a familiar twinge of pain settling uncomfortably in her chest.

Why must loving someone hurt so much?

She had lost her heart to the tawny haired Monsale the first second she had laid eyes on him. He had been thirteen, she was a mere seven. And yet, there had been something about the poorly dressed Andrew McNeal which had captivated her, long before she knew what the word love truly meant.

Her father, the Duke of Redditch had taken the orphan boy-duke under his wing the moment he arrived in London. And with his careful guidance, he had helped Monsale to slowly pull the McNeal family finances back from the brink of bankruptcy.

When he finally reached his majority, Monsale had taken over the full management of his estate and through his own efforts had taken the dukedom's wealth to a whole new level. It was rumored that he was now one of the richest men in all of Britain. More affluent than even all the major banking families.

Yet no woman had managed to capture his heart. He remained, steadfastly, and in Naomi's opinion, stubbornly, a bachelor.

Why can't you see me? I am standing right here, ready to love you.

Naomi stirred from her musings as the music stopped,

and the quadrille came to an end. They applauded the dancers. Harry downed his glass of brandy and gave her a gentle nudge.

"Why aren't you twirling around the floor this evening, Naomi? I know you love to dance."

She gave a disinterested shrug. To her way of thinking dances like the quadrille, were boring. They lacked passion. Only a waltz would tempt her, and even then, it had to be with the right partner. The only man who held her interest was the same man who paid more attention to his drink than the entertainments which the party had on offer.

"I think I may have a touch of ennui. To be honest, dear brother, if you hadn't badgered me into accompanying you this evening, I would have likely stayed at home," she replied.

It was late July, and Naomi was just about at her wits end. The social season had seen her once more left on the shelf. Certain that they couldn't ever give her what her heart desired, she had refused marriage suits from two perfectly suitable noblemen.

At six and twenty, she was in grave danger of becoming a set-in-stone, spinster, an ape leader. No other duke's daughter of her generation remained unwed.

Her father and eldest brother had both assured her, she would never be compelled to marry. And while financial security was one thing Naomi didn't have to worry about, she still hadn't managed to overcome the problem of her aching need to be wanted. To have a man in her life who truly loved her.

I've half a mind to march up to Monsale and demand that he offers for me. I would make a wonderful birthday present. Something warm and willing for him to unwrap.

Harry leaned in and nudged her once more. "Come on Naomi, cheer up. Augustus and Evangeline are arriving from France later this week. You must be eagerly awaiting their wedding ball; I know Mama and Mrs. Jones are planning a party of special magnificence."

Naomi forced a tight smile to her lips. The last thing she needed was to attend a function where love was being celebrated. And while she was happy for Gus and eager to meet his bride, she found it a struggle to dampen down her own disappointment.

She quietly admired Gus Jones's grand gesture of love. Only a man who had lost his heart completely to a woman would give up his family, his country, and go to live with her in the ruins of an old château.

How romantic. Evangeline is a lucky girl. After all that Gus has been through, he deserves to be happy.

She was still lamenting her own lack of success with love when the orchestra struck up the opening strains of a waltz. Couples quickly gathered on the dance floor once more. Naomi's pink-slipper clad feet itched to dance.

It was time to take a chance.

Nothing ventured, nothing gained.

She stepped away from her brother and came to stand in front of his friend. A scowling Monsale peered down at her from his lofty height. "Lady Naomi."

It was a familiar game; one which they had played many times before. And all with the same outcome. She had always lost.

"Your grace. Would you be so kind as to indulge me with a turn or two around the dance floor?"

His brows furrowed in their all too familiar way. Anyone would think she was asking him to ride naked along Oxford Street such was the look of surprised distaste which appeared on his face.

"Dance?"

Naomi painted a smile on her lips. "Yes. That's when people move about together in time to music. It's really quite fun. I am sure you would enjoy it immensely if you would

THE ROGUE AND THE JEWEL

just try. I am quite accomplished when it comes to the waltz, so I promise we won't look foolish."

A duke's daughter reduced to begging. What has the world come to?

The frown on his face deepened. "I don't dance."

And there it was, yet another rejection. Why did she even bother?

Because you are a silly girl who still lives in hope that he will one day see the love which shines for him in your heart. And that he will decide he cannot live without you.

Her bitter frustration spurred her on. "Didn't you hear Harry as he extolled the virtues of wedded bliss not five minutes ago? You will never find a wife if you don't socialize with the fairer sex. And if you don't have a duchess, how is the McNeal family line to continue? You have a duty to make sure that the sixteenth Duke of Monsale is born, and the title passed on."

Naomi cursed the tears which threatened. How many more times would she make a fool of herself over this man?

Monsale glanced down at the glass of brandy in his hand. "I am in no haste. When I eventually feel that it is necessary for me to take on a wife, I shall do something about it. Until then…"

He couldn't even be bothered to give her a full answer. She wished nothing more than to punch Monsale. To knock some sense into him. To make him finally see that she was more than just Harry's little sister. That in her heart of hearts she knew they were destined for one another.

She blinked back the tears, determined not to show him, or anyone else her pain.

I should not have come this evening. When am I ever going to learn that he doesn't give a damn?

"If that's the case then you should be relieved to know that women are not lining up, to become your duchess. Excuse me, your grace, I have better places to be this evening. Happy birthday, Monsale. Enjoy the rest of your night."

She gave Harry a brief nod and headed straight for the door, taking what was left of her crumbling pride with her.

🐚

Monsale lifted his brandy to his lips and took a sip, all the while his gaze lingered on the retreating figure of Lady Naomi as she walked away. The duke's daughter was feisty, headstrong, and determined.

She was also thoroughly delicious.

The way her generous breasts filled out the top of her evening gown always made his heartbeat skip to a fast clip. And the fabulous sway of her hips and ass as she moved. Even in a foul mood, she had a certain allure about her.

If only you weren't so bloody tempting.

If she had been any other woman, he might have already given up the fight and married her. But Monsale was no fool. He knew full well that the man who did eventually marry Lady Naomi Steele was signing up for a life with a stubborn wife. She had made no secret of the fact that she would want a marriage of equals. To have a say in every one of her husband's major decisions.

The mere thought made him scoff. He had never been one for any sort of connection or relationship being based on an equal footing. In his business dealings people did as he instructed. Even the other members of the RR Coaching Company, his closest friends, and partners, yielded to his demands.

He'd had almost twenty years of no one daring to question, let alone countermand his commands. His loyal steward Adan had been the first and last to try it on that fateful day in Bermuda.

Monsale had long ago realized that acquaintances and

even friends could be easily manipulated, but the woman who made it plain that she wished to be his duchess was someone he knew he could not control. Lady Naomi had grown up a duke's daughter and was used to having people listen to her. In the Steele household, her opinions carried weight. She had power and influence. And that made her dangerous to a man like him.

She will challenge me. Expect to be my equal. I can't have that with anyone.

Monsale was utterly clueless when it came to being able to handle a woman such as Naomi. He knew enough from the marriages of his fellow rogues of the road that only a rash idiot would attempt to tame a wife. Naomi wouldn't ever stand for a man to tell her what to do.

She will bite the hand off the first person who tries to put a leash on her.

During his illicit career he had battled bloody pirates and taken on both the French and British navies, but when it came to dealing with headstrong women, Andrew McNeal, Duke of Monsale hadn't the foggiest notion as to what he should do.

And yet, you still want her.

His nights had long been filled with dreams of holding Naomi naked in his arms; of her long golden locks splayed out across the sheets of his bed. Of her soft sighs of sexual completion. Of knowing that he was the only man she loved. The only one who would ever possess both her heart and body.

What on earth am I going to do about her?

"You certainly have a knack when it comes to annoying the devil out of my sister," observed Harry.

Monsale lifted his glass to his lips, surprised to discover that it was, in fact, empty. When had he finished the last of his drink?

"I don't know why she insists on asking me to dance with her, she knows I never partake," he replied.

Harry gave a knowing hum. "One day some other chap will catch Naomi's eye. Might even sweep her off her feet and offer to marry her. The question you have to ask yourself, old chap, is, are you prepared to stand by and let that happen?"

And while Naomi was no longer a fresh debutante, she was still one of the major catches of the London *ton*. Her dowry and lineage were enough to have her firmly at the top of every noble matchmaking mother's list.

Harry's remark pulled Monsale up short. Doing his best to maintain his air of vague interest, he slowly turned and met his friend's gaze. "Is there someone else in your sister's line of sight? I mean an earl or a marquis she might be prepared to settle on?"

"Who knows. But eventually, she may tire of receiving a firm no from the lips of a certain duke and decide that hearing yes from someone else is enough on which to build a life. You have been warned."

Monsale was in sudden need of another stiff drink.

Would she? Could she really choose another over me?

And what if Naomi finally did give up on him and agreed to settle down with another chap? Some gormless lesser male whom she could dominate, and who would soon bore her to tears. It was a chilling prospect, one which would see all parties living out a miserable, bitter existence.

What if I do push her patience too far? If she gives up.

He was in no particular hurry to leap into the arms of wedded bliss, but Lord Harry's words gave Monsale reason for pause. There surely had to be a limit as to what Naomi would endure from him. She was a female, and her sights had to be set on finding a husband.

What would he do if he lost her? Naomi might well be stubborn, but she was the only woman Monsale could ever imagine waking up next to for the rest of his life.

This birthday evening had seen him presented with

several unexpected gifts. The prospect of Naomi choosing another over him, the most unwelcome of them.

Perhaps I should say yes to the occasional waltz.

But that would mean handing control to Naomi. Unable to reconcile his mind to such a foreign concept, Monsale set to grinding his teeth.

Could he willingly give up any sort of power to another person?

"Impossible," he muttered.

READ KING OF ROGUES

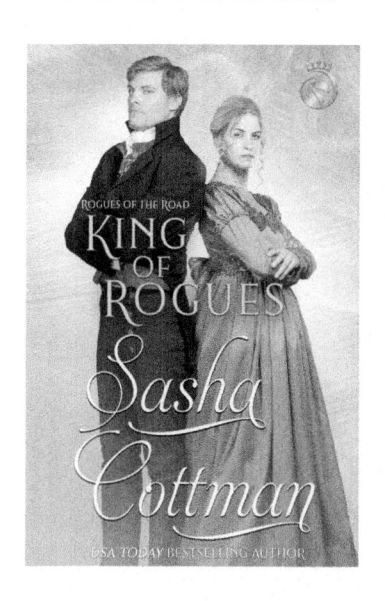

Also by Sasha Cottman

SERIES

The Kembal Family
The Duke of Strathmore
The Noble Lords
Rogues of the Road
London Lords

The Kembal Family

Tempted by the English Marquis
The Vagabond Viscount
The Duke of Spice

The Duke of Strathmore

Letter from a Rake
An Unsuitable Match
The Duke's Daughter
A Scottish Duke for Christmas
My Gentleman Spy
Lord of Mischief
The Ice Queen
Two of a Kind
A Lady's Heart Deceived
All is Fair in Love

Duke of Strathmore Novellas

Mistletoe and Kisses
Christmas with the Duke
A Wild English Rose

The Noble Lords

Love Lessons for the Viscount
A Lord with Wicked Intentions
A Scandalous Rogue for Lady Eliza
Unexpected Duke
The Noble Lords Boxed Set

Rogues of the Road

Rogue for Hire
Stolen by the Rogue
When a Rogue Falls
The Rogue and the Jewel
King of Rogues
The Rogues of the Road Boxed Set

London Lords

Devoted to the Spanish Duke
Promised to the Swedish Prince
Seduced by the Italian Count
Wedded to the Welsh Baron
Bound to the Belgian Count

USA Today bestselling author Sasha Cottman's novels are set around the Regency period in England, Scotland, and Europe. Her books are centred on the themes of love, honor, and family.

www.sashacottman.com

Facebook
Instagram
TikTok
Join my VIP readers and claim your FREE BOOK
A Wild English Rose

Writing as Jessica Gregory

Jessica Gregory
SASSY STEAMY ROMANCE

Jessica Gregory writes sassy steamy rom coms. She loves strong heroines and making her heroes grovel.

Royal Resorts

Room for Improvement

A Suite Temptation

The Last Resort

Sign up for Planet Billionaire and receive your FREE BOOK.

An Italian Villa Escape

www.jessicagregorybooks.com

Printed in Great Britain
by Amazon